"Are you alright?"

"Yea," I smiled, wincing slightly as I dropped my hand back to his waist. Kisten had a dark look on his face, his chartreuse eyes swirling. His devilish expression reminded me more of Crispin, but on him, it only excited me. Kisten moved his hands from my shoulder to my waist, a smirk on his face.

"Good." With this, he kissed me again and I moaned with both pain and desire. It felt as if he were literally setting me on fire with his touch and it excited me as much as it hurt. I could feel his fingers as he fumbled at my shirt and searing pain followed his hand as he touched my back. I merely clung to him as he stroked me, indulging in his own desires.

Dark Goddess

To Catch A Raven

To Spot A Leopard

Dark Goddess

To Catch a Raven

Yasmina Iro

iv

To Maria Croft,
For always believing in me

To my daughter Iori,
My Best Little Helper

To Vincent,
For accepting me for who I am

Prologue

"Please, take me as one of your own." I knelt on one knee and bowed my head to the vampire in front of me, allowing my long black mane to sweep the floor. I could feel his stare as he looked down at me, and I gulped quietly. I knew how outlandish my story must have sounded: it was unbelievable to most who heard it. Carefully, I uncoiled my hand across my chest to feel my heartbeat. It was there, slower that any human heart would ever beat and a constant reminder that I could no longer be considered merely human.

"Raiven," I looked up sharply as he addressed me. He had barely shifted on his couch, his blue eyes piercing into me. "I need to discuss this with my Alpha and Retainer."

"Of course." I bowed my head once more before standing, and then I left the room, closing the heavy door behind me. I let out a shaky sigh, running my hand through my kinky hair before pressing myself against the wall. It had been a long time since I had been in the presence of an Overseer, and even longer since I had asked one to be mine. My fists clenched in anger at the memory of my former Overseer, but I forced myself to slowly uncurl my fingers. I couldn't compare everyone to *him*, and I needed the protection an Overseer could offer, lest they found me again.

"Please, let him say yes." I prayed softly, closing my eyes. Although praying at this point in my long life was no more than whispering words in the wind, I couldn't seem to break the habit that had once ruled my human life. Had it not been for Mother, I would've never left that life and I would have died simply, free of the curse of my immortality and eternal loneliness.

"Damn you, Mater Vitae." I whispered, anger over taking me yet again. Although she wasn't my true mother, she was Mother to what I had become: a "dead necromancer". Cursed with the same abilities and immortality as vampires, but thanks to my necromancy, I was still human and had almost none of their weaknesses, save the blood lust.

'*How long are you going to curse her?*' The locket under my blouse grew warm as my sister's thoughts intruded onto mine and I absently grabbed the wooden artifact. It was a simple trinket, a tuareg cross that my sister had carved by hand after watching another carver in our tribe make one. It had been her pride and joy as we grew up, and now it was her home and prison. '*Concentrate on what matters right now, getting this Overseer to let you stay.*'

'*I know Sis-*'

"Raiven." I looked up to see the vampire's Retainer peek out the door. I quickly dropped my hand from the locket and followed her back inside, taking my former place standing in front of them. She curled up beside her lover on the couch, flashing brown eyes at me before tossing her red hair and throwing her arms around him. I fought the desire to gag, his Alpha obviously sharing my sentiments. He moved as far as he dared from them, sitting on the opposite edge of the couch and refusing to look at them or me.

The Overseer vampire cleared his throat to return my attention to him. With his deep blue eyes and neatly managed black hair, he was quite beautiful for a man, but anyone who could wrestle their way to being an Overseer wasn't my type. I jumped slightly when he spoke, casting my eyes to the floor. "We have discussed your proposal and have reached our decision. First, however, my Alpha has a question for you."

The shifter sighed heavily, but he did turn to me, causing me to gasp involuntarily. His eyes were chartreuse: a cat-like mix of green, yellow and brown and I knew that either he was incredibly old, far older than his appearance betrayed or had been abused by a previous Alpha. A flash of pain danced across his face, but it disappeared just as quickly.

"I apologize for the fright. Be calm, I am in control of my animal." he smiled, but it was empty and devoid of any true meaning. It was heartbreaking to see: I could tell when that smile was pure, it could light up a room. "I wanted to know why us, why The Capital?"

"I came on the advice of a friend." I answered. He muttered something about me avoiding the question, but the Overseer ignored him, stood, and stepped down in front of me. He stood over me for a moment, as if he was taking me in and I kept my gaze to the floor, not wanting to offend him.

"Do you know my name? Who I am?"

"No." I answered truthfully, as embarrassing as it sounded. Here I was, asking him to allow me into his clan, and I didn't know his name. If not for my friend's advice, I probably wouldn't have come here at all, but I was running out of time to find an Overseer on my own.

"My name is Lucius." I stared at him, astonished. He couldn't be that Lucius, not the one from her court, could he? He smiled at me, fangs appearing as he finished. "And I accept you into my clan. Welcome to Decver."

To Catch A Raven

1

"See you Tuesday, Raiven."

"Huh? Oh, bye." I waved to my co-workers as I slammed the hood of my trunk. I slid into my green Lexus and pulled away from the airport, my hands gripping the wheel tightly. It would be a good hour drive back home, and a thoughtful one. I had arrived back from NeoKansa after investigating another murder in my current case and while I enjoyed the chance to travel the country freely, I loved living in The Capital and being home more.

Besides, my current case was anything but enjoyable: always arriving too late to prevent the crime was frustrating for the whole team but especially for my boss. Any crime can be horrifying and difficult to accept but this was especially true of crimes committed by Supernaturals, which is why the case was deferred to my department.

Even before Supernaturals made themselves known a hundred years ago, they'd been committing crimes, so the FBI created a once-secret department to handle it: Division 11. Due to the large number of Supernaturals living in America, there had been a federal team and local subdivisions, each doing their best to maintain order in their area. While we weren't really the federal team anymore, Division 11 had remained largely unchanged by the war and local teams still called us in if the case was too much of a mess to handle alone.

And this case was nothing but a mess. Bodies piled up in rooms with no signs of entry, and the perpetrator was able to bypass witch spells. The list of Supernaturals that could do that was small, and each was a rare species. We had no luck so far narrowing it down to that aspect of who our killer was, and I was beginning to get more and more frustrated with the case.

Before I could dwell on it further, my phone began to ring. I knew who it was before I even began to dig around for my earpiece.

It was only so long until my boss discovered the plans I had made for his Sunday, and I doubted he was happy about it.

"What Brandon?" I answered. He scowled on the other end, clearly sharing my sentiment.

"When was I going to learn about this meeting you set up between me and that...that thing?"

"First of all, Arkrian is not a thing: he's your daughter's fiancé and you should be happy for her, even though he's a shifter." I sighed heavily, knowing this would be an unpleasant conversation. "There are far worse things to be in this world."

"Yeah, sure now he's harmless, but what about when he shifts and attacks my daughter-"

"Okay, for one, that's largely unfair towards shifters in general. They don't turn into ravaging beasts when they shift." I hated having the same argument repeatedly, and I'm sure Shannon was too, which is why she asked for my help. "We both know that. The animal is an extension of the person, not the other way around. I know-"

"Another thing, I don't want that, that...thing sleeping with my daughter when he's halfway shifted-"

"I wasn't finished yet, Boss." I growled through gritted teeth to keep certain words from spilling out. The fact that he was being unfair and extremely judgmental of Arkrian didn't matter, there are certain things you don't say to your boss. "Secondly, I know Arkrian personally, and he wouldn't do anything he knows you don't approve of. And for crying out loud, you haven't even met him! That's why I set up that damn dinner for you guys: so you could get to know him because whether you like him or not, Shannon *will* marry him."

Silence on the other end. Brandon might not have liked it, but he knew I was right. Shannon had strongly voiced that if her father refused to give her away, she would have her brother do it, who was already a part of the Supernatural community thanks to his vampire bride. It was largely Mark's secret marriage to a vampire that had Brandon upset about Shannon also marrying a Supernatural, and a shifter at that.

Brandon had lost the mother of his children to a vengeful shifter and it was something he had never truly forgiven. Although he swore that it wouldn't affect his judgement on the job, it was obvious that he still blamed all shifters and Supernaturals in general for his wife's loss. It must've seemed like a betrayal for both of his children to fall in love with non-humans, but I didn't feel that justified his behavior.

"I'm hanging up on you now, Brandon. All Shannon and I ask is that you give him half a chance, because if you don't, you're going to lose both of your children. I'd rather not see that happen." I hung up as I pulled into the driveway of my home, parking in my garage as the door opened automatically. I dragged myself out of the car, hoping to relax on my couch.

As soon as I stepped into my home however, a tugging began in the back of my mind and I groaned aloud. The Overseer was calling me toward him but I did my best to ignore the command as I stepped into the kitchen.

Searching my fridge for anything to settle my thoughts and dumping out old food, I settled on a bottle of yogurt, not wanting to put in the effort to cook. Slamming the fridge with my foot, I made my way back to my living room, where my two cats, Lira and Xris, sat waiting for me. I knew I didn't have time for them but couldn't resist the desire to rest for a few moments.

My two pretties jumped into my lap as soon as I plopped on my couch, both begging for my undivided attention. Petting with one hand and eating with the other, I gave them both attention as best I could, but my mind was elsewhere and the constant tugging wasn't helping either. Soon, both cats were meowing their disappointment in my performance.

"Well, you didn't have me for long anyway. The Overseer is calling me toward him, and I have to go pick up someone." I scoffed, pushing them both out of my lap as I stood. I wearily walked down the hall to my bedroom, groaning as I pushed the door open. Tossing my clothing on an ever-growing pile of dirty clothes, I searched through my closet, changing into a simple blue shirt and shorts. I considered doing something with my short afro, but decided against it, picking up my jacket from the bed. My cats followed my every step, begging me to stay with their purrs and meows.

Forcing myself outside and climbing wearily back into the car, I pulled away from my empty shell of a home and began cruising back toward Decver. Out of all the cities in The Capital, it was by far the biggest, but more importantly for me, it was the safest.

America had changed drastically after the 3rd World War: some argued for better, others for the worse. Gone was a centralized government, replaced by cooperating city-states each with their own human Governors and Supernatural Overseers. Governors created laws and rules that both humans and Supernaturals had to follow, while Overseers mostly dealt with keeping the needs of the various Supernaturals met. The drop from fifty-one to thirty-one states meant fewer Governors and Overseers, but also increased their responsibilities to their citizens.

The sound of my phone ringing forced me out of my thoughts and I groaned aloud once I saw the name. Although I generally made it a rule not to talk while driving, I had to make an exception for Lucius' clan and my boss. Although I wasn't high on the chain of Command, I had more freedom than most and part of my role was to be available to Lucius' people in case he couldn't be.

"Raiven speaking." I tapped my earpiece as I switched lanes.

"Hurry Raiven, it's already past eight." It was Crispin, Lucius' second-in-command. He had texted me as soon as I landed to come pick him up from his outing, since apparently Lucius wanted us for something. "Where are you?"

"On the bridge." I felt the familiar bump as I got on the bridge, switching lanes to past the slow driver in front of me. "It does take a while to get there from my house."

"I know, but can't you just speed?"

"No." I retorted. "If I get caught, I'll get a bigger ticket because I'm in a sports car and I'm not risking a ticket for your ass."

"Why, you finally made some illegal modifications to your Lexus?" he joked, and I ignored him at first. Technically, my whole make of car was outlawed: gas engines had long been replaced with electric cars and being caught driving a guzzler would result in large fines and an impounded car. However, this car had seen me to hell and back and I had brought it across the ocean with me: I would not give her up so easily.

"Of course, that's why she moves so fast." I answered sarcastically. "I'll be there soon."

"Just hurry." Turning off onto the state road, I began to move my stuff from the passenger seat. I wasn't used to having other people in my car, so any seat that I wasn't in was fair game for papers, my gun, and a plethora of trash. I picked it all up and dropped it on the backseat except for my favorite gun. I designed it, and a friend of mine who specialized in firearms built it for me. My co-workers called it The Caw and I stuffed her in her secret compartment as I pulled up next to Crispin, his gold hair glowing in the sunset and his blue eyes shining.

"Thanks Rai," he collapsed against the seat as I pulled back into traffic. "I owe you."

"De rien[1]." I brushed him off as I headed toward our Overseer, annoyed by the ever-growing traffic. "Lucius was calling me too anyway. Otherwise, you'd be stranded."

"Good. It would seem weird if you dropped me off. I hope that Eve isn't there." he sighed, closing his eyes as he slumped further in the seat. His simple shirt was unbuttoned at the top and his dark jeans hugged him tightly, but I tried not to notice as I glanced him over. Crispin was being unusually polite for once and besides that, he never shortened my name for any reason. My eyes continued drifting over him and I noticed something shiny around his wrist.

"That new?" I nodded to the watch, and then grew worried when he didn't answer. Afraid to take my eyes off the road, I reached over to touch it. The moment my fingers brushed it, I knew it was silver. I yanked it off, tossing it out the window. "God, Mikael, don't you recognize silver when you touch it?

"Sorry, I meant Crispin." I quickly corrected myself, cursing as I realized my mistake.

---

[1] French "You're Welcome"

"No, what did you call me?" Crispin leaned over to touch my arm. I flinched ever so slightly at the touch, but with him so close, there was no way he missed it. His return to normal was unfortunately quick, and I was starting to wish I had left the watch on him. "Did you call me Mikael?"

"Sorry." I muttered as we neared The Landing. I kept my eyes on the road and tried to pretend he wasn't there. "It's not like that wasn't your name but whatever."

"That was my name *before* I was turned." he put emphasis on the before as he stared at me. I refused to look at him as I parked, but after I turned off the car, he turned my face to him. I immediately pulled back from his grasp, glaring. His eyes bore into mine and I met his gaze as he spoke. "How do you know that name?"

"I know Lucius' too." I stated, willing to do anything to end his interrogation. "Sometimes I slip up with the name changes. I'll try not to dead name you again."

"Everyone knows his, but unlike him, I don't tell everyone." He tried to pull me closer, but I pulled away again, fighting the urge to slap him. He was right: under normal circumstances, I shouldn't have known his dead name. However, the situation between me and Crispin was anything but normal, and only I knew why. Before I could say anything more, Kisten came into view, saving me from the vampire's interrogation.

"There's Kisten: let's go before he gets the wrong idea." I pulled away and climbed out, thankful for his perfect timing. Crispin was about to make it evident that he wasn't done with me when Kisten stopped, staring at us. Kisten's expression was blank as he looked at us, and he seemed a little distracted.

"Does Lucius know you were out, Cris?"

"No," We answered simultaneously, then Crispin continued. "I went out on my own."

"Oh." he shrugged, his eyes lingering on me for only a moment before he looked away. A soft look flashed through his chartreuse eyes, but it passed just as quickly as it had appeared. "Well, Eve's looking for you both, so I'd hurry. Especially you, Cris."

"Where are you going?" I asked as he continued down the walk. I was surprised when he actually stopped to answer, glancing over his shoulder. His eyes softened again as they met mine and then returned to their sad and gloomy stare. My chest ached as he looked away from me again before speaking.

"Home." He shifted as he took off down the walk, rushing to get away. I watched him disappear into the darkness of the night and turned to catch Crispin walking the way Kisten had come. Silently I followed in his shadow and chastised myself for my earlier slip-up.

"Raiven!" Somewhere in my thoughts, I heard Eve's voice and I realized we had reached the back of Dream of the Incubus, or The Dream, as it was more commonly called. Lucius, being the Overseer of The Capital, owned The Landing and many nightclubs in Decver, but The Dream was one of two clubs that allowed humans and the Supernatural to mingle. By default, that also made it one of the more popular night clubs.

"Raiven, where have you and Crispin been?" She was in her security outfit and, given by her attitude, was not happy about playing babysitter at the club tonight. Lucius required all his Command to help with the business, and Eve was no exception, as much as she liked to be. Besides that, we were technically coworkers outside of the clan, and Eve never got over that I was on the federal team while she was stuck on the local. She failed to understand that I had been working with the department since its inception back in the 1930s and merely saw me as a rival in her quest for power.

The ala was glaring at me as if she wanted to eat me alive and I decided I couldn't pass up the chance to make her even more upset. Besides, Crispin had already managed to find his way on my bad side and Eve...well, she was always there.

"Well, he needed a ride back." I started, and Crispin sighed, relieved that I was telling the truth. I couldn't help my smirk as I continued. "So, I picked him up and brought him here. Then we got freaky in the car and it was *great*. You should've been there: you would have loved it."

Crispin and Eve glared at me as I smiled and shrugged. Crispin cut her off before she could say a word. "Leave it, Eve: it's not true. I did need a ride back, but I accidentally called Raiven instead of you. If you don't want me calling her, get your number changed."

'Now who's lying? At least my lie was fun.' I thought, turning away. I guess it helped to cool her down, because she turned from us, her fists curling and uncurling as she sought to control her anger. Eve's cell number was terribly similar to mine, with only the last two numbers being different and she had been encouraged to change her number several times. However, she saw it as losing to me and refused to concede.

"Anyway, both of you need to hurry. Lucius is looking for you." She stomped off into the club, her red hair waving as she left us in the darkening parking lot. Crispin and I walked down further, entering a door that would take us beneath The Landing and into the Coven. Climbing down the dimly lit stairs into the earth, Crispin suddenly stopped, and I unerringly ran into him. He whipped around like lightning, grabbed me, and pinned me to the wall with his body. With our bodies so close, I knew he felt my heartbeat quicken and I did my best to hide my anger.

"Why is it every time I touch you, your heartbeat quickens? Do I scare you or..." He leaned in close, his breath dancing across my skin. I had to fight the involuntary shudder it caused and instead I glared at him. He chuckled at my glare, clearly entertained. "Is it more?"

"Because I want your body. Now put me down." I quipped, and Crispin chuckled again, moving as if to bite me. Instead, he lightly kissed my collarbone, and it only enraged me more. I moved my leg as if to kick him, but he quickly shifted his weight to stop me. His eyes swirled with power when he looked up at me, and I knew he was using his inhuman strength to keep me pinned.

"Stop being sarcastic, Raiven. You've turned me down every time I've offered it to you."

"Then let me down and maybe I'll be honest." I stared into his eyes as he let me down, his blue eyes burning with mischief. I didn't appreciate the whole "pinning me to the wall" part of his question or the light teasing he had decided to indulge in. I rolled my shoulder a bit and cracked my neck, knowing I was only annoying him. "I'll tell you later, if I feel like it."

"In my room, then." he agreed and continued down the stairs, leaving me enraged on the steps. I felt less like telling him the truth and more like helping him to stake himself. I knew it wouldn't kill him, but it would at least incapacitate him for the rest of the night.

"Raiven, coming?" I snapped from my thoughts and jogged down the stairs to meet him. We walked down the hallway together, close enough to touch as I matched his stride. I considered smacking him for being an arrogant prick but lost the chance when we reached the living room of the underground space, Crispin opening the heavy doors.

As soon as we stepped into the room, I knew something was off. Lucius usually kept the living room fairly furnished: a couple couches, a few armchairs and a coffee station so we could gather and talk. However, now most of the furniture had been taken out: only two couches and the coffee remained, making the space seem bigger than it ever had appeared before.

"Crispin, Raiven, please sit." Lucius motioned for us to sit on the couch across from him and his guest as soon as he noticed us. Lounging on the couch beside him was a caramel-skinned vampire who was all smiles and his eyes followed us as we moved through the room. Justina, his third-in-command, stood against the far wall next to the coffee, staring off into the distance. I couldn't see her face, but the air in the room was almost suffocating, which meant she was upset about something. Lucius ignored her and continued as we sat, sitting on opposite ends of the couch. "I'd like to introduce our guest, LeAlexende, Overseer of the Southern Grove. He will be visiting with us for a few days."

"Welcome to our territory. We look forward to your graces as we bless you with ours." Ignoring the angry witch, I addressed our guest and he nodded, his already wide grin growing wider, emphasizing the oddity of his purple eyes. He tossed his dyed blonde hair as he laughed, clearly pleased with my words.

"The pleasure is indeed mine." His eyes flashed with mirth as he turned to Lucius. "She still knows the traditional greeting. An interesting one indeed, just as you said."

"Yes, indeed." The Overseer agreed and returned to addressing us. I glared at him kindly in return and he shrugged, still smiling. Sometimes Lucius' arrogance to brag about me was as annoying as Crispin thinking he owned every woman in the world. It was no wonder they got along so well. "While Alexende is in our territory, we will not use the strict Rule, but everyone of Command must remain here, save those who are out of Decver."

I groaned internally at the order but was careful not to show my disappointment on my face as I spoke. "For how long?"

"Until Monday." Three days stuck at The Dream, except for Kisten. According to Eve, he caused too much commotion when he had to stay at the Coven. Considering no one had ever seen it and the fact that Kisten was the most mild-mannered person I had ever met, I think she made it up as an excuse to not have him around to influence Lucius. Kisten never wanted to be around anyway, so I guess it was a decision that worked for both of them, which is why Lucius allowed it.

"I'll be here: I have Monday off from the office." I shrugged, doing my best to hide my annoyance. I wasn't close to most of Command and it was always awkward when I was forced to spend time with everyone else. "But I'm on call for an important case, so if it comes, I'm gone. The Rules won't keep me here anyway."

"You may leave."

I wasn't sure which way he meant it but I took it for both: I stood up to escape the room. As I walked by, Crispin grabbed my arm, forcing me to pause in my movement. At that moment, Justina glanced up with her green eyes, her deep blue hair rippling. My own power rippled through me, and I knew my eyes had grown brighter.

"Strike two, Crispin. Try me for three." I growled. I knew it was rude to fight in front of a guest, but Crispin had been working on my nerves since I picked him up. Lucius didn't say a word but the charge in the surrounding air increased, making the already dense air even harder to breathe in. Crispin glanced at Lucius, who maintained his soft smile and polite expression, which to me made him even more frightening. Crispin slowly released the grip on my arm and turned away from me.

"Crispin, I'd like to speak with you." he looked at LeAlexende and Justina. Justina left without so much as a word and LeAlexende nodded as he stood.

"I can take a hint. We can finish catching up later." The dyed Overseer waited for me to pass him. "After you."

"Merci[2]." I passed him and carefully held the door open as he walked through, making sure to close it behind us. It was about time someone talked to Crispin about his manners, or lack thereof.

"By the way, you have an interesting accent, even when you speak French. I look forward to getting to know you better... Raiven." he flashed another bright smile before walking away. Steamed by Crispin's actions and Lucius' bragging, I continued to Crispin's room and slammed the door. On the other side, I heard someone mutter about me being inconsiderate, but I didn't care in the least. I leaned against the door, the weight of my evening trying to drown me.

Sighing heavily, I forced myself up from the heavy wood and collapsed into his armchair, closing my eyes as I waited.

---

[2] French "Thank You"

2

"Raiven, is that you?" I opened my eyes as Justina invited herself into the room. A glance at the clock told me I had only been asleep for a short while and I rubbed my eyes as she closed the door. If it had been anyone else, I would've helped them see their way out: however, Justina was higher on the food chain here and on top of that, I actually liked her. "Why are you in Cris' room?"

"He wanted to talk in his room." I sighed, relaxing back into his armchair. Justina sat on the bed across from me, her expression showing how much she didn't believe me. I shrugged, sinking lower into the chair. "I'm finally going to tell him the truth so he'll leave me the hell alone."

"Which one?" She joked lightly, until she realized the annoyed look in my eye. Her face turned serious and her voice dropped in volume. "Oh, that one... Are you sure you're ready? That he's ready?"

"The sooner, the better. I'm so tired of him and besides... I need to do this. For me." I closed my eyes, reliving old memories. The witch said nothing, waiting patiently for me to continue. "He'll be fine. He's turned into such a womanizer that I doubt it'll bother him that much. I'm the one who's been carrying this."

"You've carried your guilt long enough. Time for you to let go." Justina assured me, studying me. Then: "Did you know that when I first saw your face, I thought you were so beautiful. It's not common to see someone with dark skin and bright green eyes and your hair was so beautiful and unique. It's a shame you had to cut it short."

"Oh, don't you start it too: everyone has been complaining about that. We both know I was sick of all that hair and besides, your eyes are greener than mine." I pointed out, rubbing my hand over my short afro and she laughed. She stood, causing me to rise from my seat as well.

"Ой бай[3], I am Russian, Rai. Green eyes are a part of what I am." She kissed my forehead lightly, before kissing me gingerly on the lips. I particularly enjoyed kissing Justina, but for her it was a gesture of closeness and trust. I had learned long ago to accept them as merely that and to quell any thoughts of it being more. "But you are not and that makes you special. I can see you don't need to be alone tonight: Lodge with me and I will keep you company. Far better to sleep with a live body than a dead one."

"Don't I know it." I jokingly answered, reluctantly letting her hand slip from mine, and I fell back onto Crispin's chair as she left. I closed my eyes again as she gently closed the door, my thoughts trailing to the years I had with Crispin before he was turned. Then, way back then, he was kind, sweet, and thoughtful, just like...

"Raiven." I barely moved as he walked in and closed the door silently behind him. I ran my hand over my hair again, keeping my gaze on Crispin as he sat on his bed, studying him, reading him. Hating what being turned had done to him.

Some say that being turned revealed a person's true nature, but that's a lie people tell themselves to feel better about the truth. Many Supernaturals had no choice about their nature: they were born that way and had to find ways to deal with it. Being undead was unnatural, and it can, it does, change who you are. It was impossible to cross over and come back the same person and a slight shudder ran through me as I tried to clear my thoughts.

"What did Lucius want?" I asked softly, Crispin scoffing in response.

"To 'remind' me that I'm not supposed to make a scene in front of guests." He repeated sarcastically, making air quotes as he spoke. "Honestly, I think you made more of a scene than me."

"You started it and you damn well know it." I could feel the long rant boiling in my throat, but I forced myself to swallow it down. "Do you want to know why I know your name or not?"

"Well, I'm going to guess someone told you." He looked at me coyly, crossing his legs as he leaned back on his bed. Crispin was still

---

[3] Russian "Geez" or "Oh my"

handsome, his golden hair always somehow falling exactly right around his shoulders. I found myself tracing the stark line of his collarbone with my eyes, following the line between his chest. His top buttons were still open, showing the muscle he had never had before being turned. His dark pants did little to hide his physique but despite the changes, I couldn't help but trace with my eyes what I had once touched with my hands.

Crispin cleared his throat to get my attention, causing me to jump slightly and raise my eyes to his. His face held a devilish grin, and he lifted his hand to his chest, enticingly tracing the exposed skin there. He knew I had been staring at him and I snorted, turning away from his display.

"Yes, someone did. You." I said plainly, and Crispin laughed, throwing his head back for gravitas. I waited until he decided to stop being dramatic and to see that I wasn't kidding. He let out a loud breath, leaning forward on his elbows as he spoke.

"I think I'd remember if I did."

"It was before you were turned." I closed my eyes, sighing heavily as I tried to decide how honest I wanted to be. "You and I were once close friends, maybe more than that. We had met at a party and I guess hit it off well. I know your memories of before are spotty at best, but..."

"I can't say my recollection is the best, but I think I'd remember you: you are quite unusual after all and an exquisite beauty, even now." Crispin smiled, his fangs appearing as he gazed at me. He undressed me with his eyes as I had done him, and I didn't appreciate the look. After all my time here, any other person would have given up pursuing me, but to Crispin, he saw it as a challenge and it only made him that much more determined to have me. "You are much, much older than me, so you would've already been changed by time you met me."

"I was, and the memories might surface someday, if I stay here." I sighed internally as I mused. "We spent a lot of time together back then, in the comfort of each other's embrace. Then-"

"Oh?" The dark hint that entered his expression as he interrupted me was enough to make me stand and move for the door. However, he was faster and managed to pin me to it, preventing me from leaving.

Crispin pressed himself into me, placing his hand over mine on the handle as he kept me pinned to his door. He slid his free hand down my back, gingerly lifting the edge of my top and tracing the skin above my shorts, teasingly playing with the small of my back. I had to fight the desire to arch my back towards him and tried to ignore his playful touch as he whispered into my ear, his voice deep and sultry.

"Well, maybe you should use your embrace to remind me. Perhaps I might remember if I had a taste." I closed my eyes, focused on my anger and whipped around sharply. He must not have expected me to react so violently, because he was easily tossed back by my movement. His eyes showed shock for a moment, before returning to their devilish intent. "It's an honest suggestion, Raiven."

"Back then, my embrace meant something to you. *I* meant something to you." I spat, taken aback by my tone. I was angry, but I was also... hurt. Hurt in a way I thought I had long overcome. "Enough that you wanted to marry me.

"But now that you've turned, commitment means nothing to you. You act as if every woman is yours and it is a privilege to sleep with you. Multiple partners are fine, but you don't have partners: you have one-night lovers." I turned away from his unreadable expression, my anger fuming. "I *hate* seeing what you've become, knowing that it's my fault. That I couldn't protect you when you needed me the most. That's why I avoid you, why I hate being near you. I knew you as a kind caring soul, who would've never used another person.

"But Mikael is dead and instead, we all have Crispin, with nobody to blame but me." With that, I left the room, slamming the door again. I thought I heard him softly call my name, but I ignored this, heading for Justina's room. My gait slowed as I realized I was approaching my door and I paused as I reached it. I slowly fingered the raven carved into the wood, my anger beginning to fade now that I was no longer near the vampire.

Slowly, I went inside, pausing in the doorway of my dark room. My eyes drifted through the darkness before resting on my vanity against the far wall, just visible with the light from the hallway. Turning on the light near the door, I slowly made my way to my small makeup desk and sat down.

I reached for an ornate jewelry box, opening it to reveal the various jewels and gems that had been gifted to me over the years. My eyes rested on a single ring, the reason I had entered my room and been drawn to the desk. It was a beautiful virgin rainbow opal, set in silver with small diamonds framing the jewel. A longing for the original owner rose in me as I stared at the ring and I leaned forward at my desk as I carefully lifted it up.

'Why do you want that?' My sister's consciousness suddenly spoke, making me jump in my seat. I grabbed the wooden locket that housed my sister's soul as it grew warm under my shirt. It was a relic of a time long gone and would make any museum curator or collector jealous of its antiquity. *'I thought you said you'd never wear it since you can't be with him.'*

"I know." I gazed into the beautiful stone again and this time, I could see his face, hear his laugh. I looked up into the mirror, seeing the dark-skinned beauty that stared back at me. I was abnormal, never to be accepted as a human or Supernatural. A prize to some, a threat to others, but he had treated me like a treasure, an equal. "I know, I just..."

My voice trailed off as I spoke and I felt my sister's disdain as she scoffed.

'Miss him? Raiven, you barely knew him. You miss your idea of who he was.'

"Yea... I know, I know." I carefully put the ring back where it belonged and, choosing a different one, slowly stood up from my desk. "Go back to sleep, you shouldn't waste energy right now."

'Fine. Be well, Raiven.' I quietly left my room as her consciousness faded and I continued to Justina's room. The room was already dark when I stepped inside, and I could hear Justina's soft breathing as she slept. Once inside the dark room, my day pressed on me once more and I heeded the call of rest. After slipping

on a black gown, I collapsed beside her in the bed, sleep claiming me.

3

I awoke late the next day with Justina's strong arms around me and her cool breath on my neck. The scent of vanilla wafted up my nostrils and I realized the being beside me wasn't Justina. I quickly sat up and Aurel laughed as he released me.

"Well, good afternoon. I thought you were going to sleep all day." he sat up as well, revealing that he was nude from the waist up. "By the way, I like the ring. It's gorgeous on your petite hands. Whoever got it for you picked it exactly right."

He reached for my hand to examine it and I allowed him, a small smile starting on my face. One of Aurel's many hobbies was to collect jewelry from the past and he had quite the collection. After all, he had been collecting for the past five hundred years and was jealous of every piece I owned. After a while, he spoke again, the awe obvious in his tone. "This is ancient, really ancient. Mesopotamia?"

"Yeah, a good friend got it for me for one of my birthdays." I smiled, loving Aurel's expression as he studied the ring. I glanced around the room for its owner but saw no sign of her. "Where's Justina?"

"Dunno." he shrugged, looking up and releasing my hand. "She left and told me to watch you. Made me give her a bloody oath."

"So, you decided to climb in bed with me, right?" I joked as he laughed again. It was a true laugh, something most vampires couldn't pull off and a sound I enjoyed hearing from him.

"You know you liked it." he tickled me, causing me to thrash on the bed, trying to escape his hands. I managed to get my hand to Aurel's only ticklish spot, and now it was his turn to writhe and laugh under my touch as I reveled in my victory.

"Stop, stop." he begged, and I conceded. He let out a happy sigh, closing his eyes and wiping away his pink tears. It wasn't uncommon for vampire tears to be pink, as most failed to keep themselves hydrated due to lack of need. A hydrated vampire would cry clear tears, similar to the living, but it was rare to find one who could.

With him lying there, looking so helpless, I couldn't help myself: I started tickling him again. This time, however, he caught my hands and opened his eyes. His eyes bore into mine and I forced myself to look away, clearing my throat to try to break the tension. Aurel's eyes were a brilliant hazel and his strong face was always wildly framed by his dark orange curls. His gaze bore deeply into me as I tried to pull my hands away and he stopped me, pulling me closer to him instead.

"Raiven," he reached to stroke my cheek and I pulled back, not wanting him to touch me. Aurel's feelings toward me had begun to shift and while he had yet to verbally admit it, I knew he would soon. I didn't feel more than friendship for him and I drew in a deep breath, steeling myself for what I needed to say.

"Aurel?"

"Yes?" his voice was so soft, so full of his desire for me that it caused the words to get caught in my throat. Before I could force myself to continue, I was saved by Crispin's and Justina's voice in the hallway. We couldn't let them see us like this: as fate would have it, everyone believed that we hated each other, and it had helped our friendship grow without the bother of rivalry from Aurel's other consorts. I could see in his eyes that he wanted to pretend that we had a fight, and a fight was the furthest thing from my mind.

"You're so self-centered." he hissed as he stood out of the bed. He was trying to make me angry, and he knew the words to say to get me going. "You don't care for anyone else besides yourself."

"I'm self-centered? Have you looked in the mirror?" I scoffed, standing as well. "You never seem to care about how I feel. You walk off like nothing happens, like what you say and do doesn't affect anything. It does, Aurel, it affects everything."

"Affects everything? You act like I don't exist half the time Raiven." Aurel's eyes flashed for a moment as he spoke, and I realized he wasn't making up something to make it seem like we were arguing. He was...being honest. "You say we're friends but all you do is push me away. You never want to spend any time with me unless you have to. Do you even want to hang around me, or do you just do it out of pity?"

"Maybe because I don't want to hurt you, you idiot." I snorted, moving away from the bed to Justina's armchair. I gripped the back tightly as I scowled at the vampire. "Does forcing yourself on me make you any better? Maybe the reason I don't spend time with you is because you always guilt trip me about it. To me, you're no better than Mother, wanting to add me to another one of your collections."

Surprised flitted across Aurel's face at me comparing him to Mother and I immediately regretted my words. Comparing anyone to Mater Vitae was a great insult, and the words had flown out of my mouth without thought. Upon recognizing the hurt and pain in his eyes, I tried to apologize.

"Aurel, I'm sorry, I didn't-"

"Of course not. You never do." He walked by me without looking up and pushed his way past Crispin and Justina as they walked in the door. I collapsed down into the chair, cradling my face between my hands as I mentally chastised myself for my hasty words. Justina looked after Aurel as he left, turning a quizzical expression to me.

"What happened?"

"We were fighting like usual, what else is there to know?" I fought to keep my vitals in check so they wouldn't catch the small lie I had implemented into my explanation. I looked up from my hands, looking at the pair. "Why did you leave me with him anyway?"

"I needed to get Crispin and I didn't want to leave you alone. Plus, I thought you...well, obviously I was wrong." Justina shook her head disapprovingly as I tried to change the subject.

"What did you two talk about?"

"That's private." She glanced at him and I didn't like the look they shared. It not only confused me, but it was if they had a whole conversation with that one look.

"Is there something I should know about?" I didn't do much to hide the suspicion in my voice as I spoke, pulling my legs into the chair.

"No." Crispin answered, a little too quickly. I was still suspicious but decided not to push it as he continued. "I have permission to leave but I have to be back before Alexende and Lucius wake up."

"And? I care because?" I glanced at the clock above her bathroom, which read a little after one. Elder vampires could escape death after 2pm while it took younger ones longer to wake. Justina must've used her magic to wake Crispin and Aurel early and I glanced at her. She was looking away from me, her expression somber.

"And, I need a ride and I want to show you something." Crispin smiled mysteriously, and Justina looked up to shoot him an angry glance. I didn't hesitate with my answer.

"No."

Crispin looked ready to argue when Justina stopped him and looked at me, a pleading look in her eyes. "Raiven, please."

I was even more confused by Justina sticking up for him. Justina had only ever approved of my telling him because she knew I hated keeping it a secret. Justina was the first to realize how much it bothered me not to have it in the open and offered me an outlet. Witches were also intuitive and sensitive to others in that way and I was always grateful for her support. I met Justina's gaze and I wasn't sure what I saw there, but it was enough for me to relent.

"Fine. Just leave while I dress."

"Sure." Justina cut Crispin off and pushed him out the door. I grabbed a pair of dark pants and a blue shirt, but I dressed near the door so I could hear their conversation. Justina's door never truly closed anymore due to a physical altercation between me and a suitor who would "have Justina or die". I granted him the latter.

"Don't play with her Cris." Justina warned, her voice low and heavy, almost as if she were preparing to cast. "You'll pay for it. She'll make sure you hurt for it. You just need to tell her the truth."

"I won't." he promised lightly and even through the door I could tell he didn't mean it. She obviously did too as Justina sighed heavily.

"You will, I know it." She sounded defeated. "You will never change."

"And you'll never trust me. I won't play with her that badly." Crispin laughed softly and it sounded like he moved closer to her. "Let me have at least a little fun."

Justina never got to reply because I opened the door at that moment and Crispin quickly stepped back. I sighed, still not trying to hide my displeasure. "I'm as ready as I'll ever be."

"Good." he linked my arm in his and we walked down the dark Coven hallway into the way-too-bright sunshine. He held out his hands for the keys, and I merely stared at his hand as if it were a foreign object.

"I'm driving." He said matter-of-factly, and I shifted my gaze to his face. A small smiled creeped across my features, but I fought to keep it back as I crossed my arms across my chest, meeting Crispin's gaze.

"Says who?"

"Raiven, I don't have time for this." he came up to me and glared, his eyes swirling with power. Crispin knew well enough that he could not scare me with a power struggle, and I finally surrendered to my smile as I kept my eyes on his face.

"Time for what?" I asked sweetly, and he reached as if to push me back into the wall and take the keys by force. Part of me wanted him to touch me, as I still wanted to pay him back for the night before. Instead, he wised up and stepped back from me, a smug smile taking the place of his glare.

"If you'd rather stay here, I have no problem with that." He started back towards the Coven. "Even better, I can get Aurel to come up here and keep you company instead. Maybe he'll add you to his harem since you don't want me."

"Whatever." I tossed him the keys and climbed in the car, waiting impatiently as he climbed into the driver's seat. "Where are we going?"

"What fun would that be?" He leaned over and kissed me before I could react. After it occurred to me that this was strike three for him, I slapped him into his door. He actually had the audacity to grin at my retaliation, and then I realized he kissed me in order to get a reaction.

"You must have enjoyed it to slap me that hard."

Seething and resisting the desire to slap him again, I turned away from him as we left The Landing. As my anger passed, my mind floated to Aurel. Guilt gripped my mind and chest as I remembered how I had hurt him by comparing him to Mater Vitae. It was the worst thing I could've said, considering all the horrible things Mother had done when she controlled Supernaturals and those in her court.

"Where are we?" I leaned forward as we pulled into what appeared to be a public garden. Such gardens were common now, making it easier for people to plant and care for their own plot of flowers or vegetables. Crispin merely smiled, getting out and handing me the keys.

"Just set your watch for 2:15." He still refused to answer me as he started for the garden's entrance. I set my watch and watched him walk away, leaning against my car. He managed to get pretty far before he realized I wasn't following. Our game resumed as he turned back to face me. "C'mon Raiven."

"Why?"

"You'll see." He stood there facing me, arms crossed. Stubborn, I equally crossed mine and stared at him. For a while neither of us moved and I took a moment to glance at my watch. If I could hold him for a few more minutes, I wouldn't have to worry about whatever it was he wanted to show me. Then suddenly, he tossed his hair, flashing a stream of gold. "Oh, well, let's go. I'll just tell Justina that we drove here for nothing."

I was intrigued by his mention of Justina but refused to move for a moment longer. Crispin waited to see if his words had affected me before he started walking towards the car. I waited until he was within arm's length before I walked past him, twisting so he couldn't touch me.

"I knew you'd give in." he grinned behind me as he followed.

"Don't get cocky." I warned. "I only gave in because if I didn't, it would've been a waste of my gas. It's hard enough to come by."

"True, true." he nodded, only pretending to agree. I turned around and slapped him again: half for the sarcasm I didn't appreciate, half because he was so cocky.

"Raiven." He cradled his cheek as he smirked, his whining tone not matching his expression.

"You'll live."

"I'm hurt." He gasped, but he grabbed my hand. I snatched it back, hissing as he walked past me. I growled as I began following him, wanting this outing over with.

'Raiven.' My sister's voice rose in my mind again as she responded to my annoyance. 'Who are you with?'

'Say hello to the new improved Mikael, now known as Crispin: the cockiest S-O-B you'll ever meet.' The locket grew warm under my shirt and out of habit, I reached up to grab it. Once I realized Crispin was watching me, however, I stopped. 'Stay low, sis, or you'll be discovered again.'

'If you don't want to be with him, then leave. No need to get so worked up.' I began to refute her statement but she slipped away before I could respond. I looked up as Crispin moved aside a curtain of yellow jasmines and he motioned me in as I marveled at the beauty of the garden. It was filled with a variety of flowers, all of which were beautifully in bloom. However, it was more than that: this was my garden, a garden I had tended to what seemed like a lifetime ago.

"I knew you'd like it." I turned to glare as Crispin spoke. He raised his hands in defense and he was strangely sincere. "Not like that: you used to have a garden like this, I think. It's where I pro... was going to propose. Never mind, that's not important."

Crispin came closer to me and I instinctively stepped back. He sighed: all his usual playfulness gone from his eyes. He gingerly touched one of the petals, looking at it softly before returning his gaze to me. For a brief moment, he was like his old self again, gleaming in the sunlight as he helped care for the garden he thought so dutifully reflected me.

"I planted this the year you came. I'm not much for gardens now, and I didn't really know why, but I just felt compelled to." His newly softened expression looked strange to me, as if it didn't belong to him. The man standing in front of me seemed more like Mikael than Crispin and I couldn't help but step closer to him, my heart filling with an ache I thought I no longer had. "I know you probably don't believe me when I say this, but... I do appreciate you telling me. I don't remember and I probably never will, but-"

Crispin moved quickly and wrapped his arms around me, holding me close. Before I could object or react, he leaned down and kissed me, but this no longer felt like Crispin. I couldn't help myself as I wrapped my arms around him to pull him closer.

I had never forgiven myself for allowing Mikael to be turned and never realized how much I still missed him. His gentle, uncertain kisses, the soft tenderness of being in his arms...and blood. His lips had the tainted taste of blood and whereas I had missed it in the car earlier, now I tasted it faintly on his lips. My mental cage to keep my thirst at bay started to break down as I kissed him deeply to taste the sweet liquid.

"Raiven," his voice was muffled from the force I was now pushing on him, almost forcing him to the ground. He tried his best to shift his arms to push me away, but I tightened my grip to keep him still. I was starting to lose grasp on where I was and who I was with; all that mattered was the blood in his mouth and getting more of it. I pulled away from his lips and started for his throat, my fangs extending from my mouth.

"Raiven!" Crispin managed to untangle himself from me and pushed me into a bed of roses. "What in hell is wrong with you?!"

I almost sprung back up, wanting more but his push allowed me to regain enough control to slam the addiction behind its steel doors. I breathed in the scent of the flowers to calm myself as the lusty glow left my eyes and my fangs disappeared back into my mouth.

"Sorry," I muttered, somewhat embarrassed as I stood. "It has been a while since...since I've lost control like that..."

"I know." The cockiness was still gone, replaced by a kind man. At least, he still looked less cocky and more concerned. "We

have to wait a week after we've fed before being near you. But it's been nearly two weeks since my last feeding."

"The taste, oh, the taste was still there." A faint glow began in my eyes as I thought about the kiss, but I pushed it back. "I've held off my lust for months: at this point merely thinking about it sets me off. Oh gods, you tasted so sweet-"

"Look, Raiven. I'm sorry." He breathed. I was so surprised by it that it overcame the addiction that had tried to take over my mind again. Crispin didn't apologize, not even to Lucius and definitely not to a woman. "I didn't bring you out here to play with you, despite what you may think. Honestly, I need..."

Crispin paused, looking away from me, pouting at a bed of gardenias. I wasn't sure what to make of what was happening as I looked over the vampire. Crispin turned back as if he was finally ready to speak when my watch began to scream. It started a scream that would have made a banshee proud as the alarm went off, declaring the time.

Glancing at Crispin, I left the garden and began for my car. Crispin walked faster and reached it first, walking to the driver's side. I didn't fuss as I tossed him my keys and hopped into the passenger seat. Whether I wanted too or not, we had to return to The Dream before Lucius and LeAlexende woke up for the day or the Rules would punish us both. As Crispin sped us back, I couldn't help but wonder what he had wanted to say in the recreated garden.

4

I leaned against my car as Crispin walked into the Coven, disappearing into the darkness below. If we walked in together, it would've raised so many unnecessary problems with Eve that I didn't want to deal with. I could be a smart ass when I wanted to, but there were times when I didn't want to bother.

Now was one of them as my mind drifted back to the garden once the door had closed behind him. He had seemed different and his demeanor left me confused. Sincerity was not in Crispin's vocabulary and I had never seen him be so soft with anyone. A part of me wanted to believe that Mikael was still in him somewhere, but another argued that he was no longer that person. I had always agreed with the latter, but now, I wasn't sure what to think.

A few minutes after Crispin disappeared, Aurel came storming up the stairs, slamming the door into the wall. Barely glancing my way, he slammed his fist into the concrete, cursing in French. Aurel wasn't the type to speak French, so I knew he had to be really upset over whatever had happened. He had still failed to put on a shirt apparently, his alabaster skin practically blinding in the afternoon sunlight.

"Aurel," I tried to get his attention, my pride screaming at me. If looks could kill, I would've died ten times over from the glare he gave me. I frowned, displeased with his reaction. "What's your problem?"

"What's my problem?" Suddenly he was in my face and vanilla flooded my mind until I wanted to push him back before the sweet scent suffocated me. "Oh, nothing, just that Eve is being an annoying bitch and I want to rip her guts out!"

"Well, sorry, that's not really news around here." I didn't like him taking his anger out on me, especially when I had nothing to do with it. Most of us thought Eve abused her position as Lucius' Retainer, but that was hardly my fault. I realized Eve probably had taken a jab at Aurel's harem again, something he was very touchy about. "*I* was trying to apologize."

The angry lines left his face, but he didn't move, his orange curls bouncing. He looked at me with genuine confusion as he spoke, still leaning over me. "Apologize for what?"

"What I said earlier." I muttered, looking away. "I didn't mean to say it like that or to compare you to Mother. I don't really think you're like her. You're pushy at times, but you genuinely care about others. Like with your harem, and that's something she could never understand."

Surprised by my words, he smiled at me, putting his hands on my car, and pinning me to the hood with his body. Aurel leaned down as if to kiss me and I turned away from him. He instead placed a light kiss on my cheek, lips barely brushing against my skin. He pulled back slightly, his eyes now looking at me softly.

"Don't worry about it luv, I'm over it." Aurel grinned at me and I chuckled softly.

"Didn't take long."

"What can I say? I just can't stay mad at you." He looked ready to say something else but instead he leaned his head down, placing his neck close to my mouth. I could smell the fresh blood pulsing beneath the skin, and I had to push him away. After my encounter with Crispin, my addiction was already barely under control and I looked at him with horror. He looked at me surprised, confused by my refusal of him. "What's wrong?"

"You've fed today. You need to leave." I turned away from him, trying not to think about the fresh blood now running through his veins. The red, sweet blood that filled his luscious body, waiting for me to indulge. I grabbed my arm as it shot out to grab him, digging my nails into my own flesh. "You need to leave now. You know better than to come around me after feeding."

"Raiven," His voice whined with how much he wanted to stay, but I knew it wasn't safe. I shook my head, refusing to look at him.

"Leave now, Aurel, or I will make you leave. Don't come near me." I found it difficult to speak as my fangs tried to reveal themselves and I fought to keep them in my mouth. After a long silent pause, I heard Aurel walk away and breathed a sigh of relief as the door to the Coven closed. I opened my eyes to the afternoon sun and tried to control my blood lust.

"You okay, Rai?" I looked down to see Kisten step out of his silver mustang. He was dressed up with a blue silk shirt and black dress pants, and a simple gold chain around his neck. His hair was combed back into a slick back style, with a few strands refusing to obey and hanging in his face. I could almost hear his blood pumping beneath his skin as he closed the car door. I dug my nails into the hood of my car, the screeching sound almost enough to drown out the lust.

"Go away, don't come near me." I growled through semi-closed lips and I closed my eyes. I was close to crying as I heard Kisten walk towards me. *'Please, Kisten, I don't want to...'*

Suddenly, I felt a sharp pain in my hand and I opened my eyes to see Kisten piercing my skin with his sharp claws. Kisten was such an old and experienced shifter that he could shift any part of himself that he wanted to independently and his hand and forearm bore his beautiful leopard spots. Despite the blood his claws were now drawing from me, I felt an urge to pet the soft fur gracing his skin.

Before I could ask why he had scratched me, Kisten forced my hand to my mouth, allowing me to taste my own blood. As soon as the taste hit my mouth, all thoughts of wanting blood faded. The cold metallic taste was nothing like the sweet taste I craved and was familiar with. It was like jumping into a cold shower: I sobered up quickly and the addiction faded to its usual dark pit. I looked at Kisten in surprise as he released me, still holding my hand to my mouth, and letting the blood flow in. He smiled at me softly, shifting his hand back to being human.

"You never thought of that?"

"I..." I wanted to give some sort of excuse, but I couldn't think of anything to say. Kisten's eyes lit up with mirth, and I saw the corners of his mouth twitch up as he worked to hold in his laughter. I took my hand out of my mouth, and tried my hardest to look upset, fighting my own smile. "Well, why in the world would I ever do that to myself?"

"It seemed like a good idea. Would be bad if you wanted to drink your own blood." He shrugged, turning to walk back to his car. "Give me a moment to get my kit and I'll treat you."

I said nothing and merely watched as he dug through his trunk to find his first aid kit. As the Alpha, Kisten took taking care of his pack seriously and it was obvious why him and Lucius were both good friends as well as connected as Overseer and Alpha. His kit was fitted to treat any kind of shifter and almost any possible wound that could be sustained, whether from each other or Hunters.

He came back with a large roll of gauze as well as a needle and thread and I winced when I noticed. Kisten set down the supplies and reached for my hand. I instinctively pulled it away, looking at the needle. Kisten followed my gaze and gave me an incredulous look.

"Are you seriously going to tell me you are afraid of needles?"

"I'm not afraid, just..." The words faded and Kisten sighed, taking my uninjured hand in his. He gently stroked the back of my hand before quickly kissing it, the gesture burning my skin.

"Uncomfortable? Because of Mother?" He whispered, and I nodded, wanting to press his hand to my face, wishing I could relax in his arms. He kissed the back of my hand again before releasing it and gently touching my face with his fingertips, the closest he would get to caressing me. "You know I know what I'm doing. It'll be a quick stitch and taken out tomorrow once you've healed."

"I know." I closed my eyes as he got to work. Kisten was a doctor and worked at the local hospital, specializing in treatment of Supernaturals. It was kind of unfair to his patients, since technically, he oversaw so many of them, but I think it was how Kisten preferred it. Working at the hospital gave him the authority that he needed to take care of his people, no matter the circumstance.

"There, done." Kisten patted my freshly dressed wound and I opened my eyes. Green met chartreuse as we looked at one another and, unable to resist, I reached out to touch his face with my uninjured hand. His hand caught mine however, and he held it awkwardly for a moment, before picking up my bandaged hand and pressing it to his face instead. He kept his eyes locked on mine and I felt as if my heart would beat right out of my chest.

"This isn't what I want." I sighed, dropping my hand in frustration. Kisten dropped his as well, gathering up his materials from the hood of my car. He held out his hand and I accepted it as he helped me down.

"I know Raiven, but I can't hurt you again." Kisten's expression resumed its gloomy stare and my heart sank. It had been a long time since I had allowed anyone into my heart, but Kisten...he was different. Kisten had been so lonely for so long, it was as if he didn't remember what it was like to be loved by another person. I never went long without physical comfort, but before me was a man who had not touched another being in more than two centuries. I never questioned him about it, but I wanted to know why he had chosen to be by himself for so long.

"C'mon Raiven, you need to get ready." Kisten's voice drew me from my thoughts and I watched as he checked his shirt for bloodstains. It dawned on me that he wasn't supposed to be at the Coven while LeAlexende was in town and I gave him a confused look.

"Actually Kisten, why are you here? I thought yo-" I was interrupted by the door behind me slamming open, and I turned to see LeAlexende and Lucius bursting up the stairs, carrying someone between them. Lucius turned to look at us and relief flooded his eyes when he saw Kisten. It was then when I noticed the dark blue hair and the constant dripping blood from my friends' body.

"Kisten, it's Justina, she-" Lucius didn't get to finish as I scooped up my friend from the Overseers and deposited her into the backseat of Kisten's car, sliding in with her. Kisten quickly got into the driver's seat and gave a quick nod to Lucius, who simply nodded back. The other two moved to Lucius' car as Kisten peeled out of the parking lot and sped down the road. As he flew to make it to the hospital, I held Justina's hand tightly. She was still alive, but barely and I prayed that we would make it in time.

5

I waited impatiently in the waiting room with the two Overseers, Kisten tending to Justina's injuries. As soon as we arrived, the staff backed out of Kistens' way, allowing him to place Justina on an empty gurney. They recognized who Justina was immediately and merely rushed him off to surgery, allowing him to choose the doctor who assisted him.

She was badly torn up, almost as if she had been hacked by several blades or slashed many times by claws. All Lucius and LeAlexende could tell me was that they woke up from Death to her screaming and when they tried to enter her room with Crispin, they found themselves unable to open the door, which should have been impossible. Finally, Crispin used his power to rip the door off its hinges and they found Justina in that state, barely conscious from blood loss. Lucius then ordered Crispin to remain behind and to check on the other witches in the Coven as well as enlist the help of his fourth, Liel.

I called my boss as soon as Kisten took Justina into surgery and asked him to bring one of the agents with him to the hospital. Although not a perfect fit, the MO fit our current case too well for me to ignore it. I wanted to ask Justina what happened, but I knew that Brandon also needed to hear whatever she had to say.

"What's the status, Raiven?" Brandon walked in all business with Christopher, one of our better agents, in tow. Lucius and Brandon exchanged a cursory nod before my boss turned back to me.

"Justi... The victim is currently in surgery. It's Justina, third to Lucius and a powerful witch in her own right." I tried my best to remain calm and professional as I recounted what the Overseers had told me and Chris dutifully wrote it all down. Brandon sighed heavily after asking a few more questions of the pair, but they were unable to provide any more information.

"I'll be honest, this is a breakthrough if it's related and she survives." He muttered, stretching his neck. "We've never had a survivor before, although I find it strange that she was alone. Usually there are multiple people in a room before our suspect attacks, in order to claim as many victims as possible."

"That would be impossible in my Coven." Lucius offered, and we turned to face him. "Never more than three to a room for extended periods of time, and larger groups must take place in open areas with no doors."

"Why such a rule?"

"Infighting for one. That many species in a space can fuel some century old tensions." I answered, crossing my arms across my chest. "But also because of Mo... Mater Vitae."

"You mean the one who made Supernaturals?" Brandon asked and I looked to Lucius to explain. Lucius gave me an exasperated glance before returning his attention to my boss. "What does she have to do with groups?"

"If too many Supernaturals gather at once, Mater Vitae can...manifest if she wants." Lucius explained cautiously and it was obvious from his tone he didn't want to talk about it. "She...is not favorable to have around, so most Overseers have similar rules."

"Hmmm, explains why many of the murders included quite a number of humans..." Chris mused, flipping through his notebook. "But what role do Supernaturals play into his choice of victims? He doesn't seem to be going after a species, just numbers. But then why would he go after Justina on her own?"

"Unless..." An idea started into my head and I didn't like where my thoughts were leading me. "They knew what she could do and wanted to take her out first."

"Could do?" Brandon gave me a strange look and Lucius' eyes lit up with worry. He almost seemed to be panicked, an expression I was not used to seeing on his face. LeAlexende gently touched his back, giving a friendly rub.

"No. No one could know that." He stammered and looked between his hands to the floor. "We never told anyone, no one knows except the highest members of Command."

"Knows what?" Brandon asked again, clearly confused and getting frustrated as LeAlexende did his best to comfort his friend. I looked to Lucius for confirmation and he met my eyes with worry. I understood his concern, but I needed to explain everything to Brandon.

'*It could help us catch the one who did this.*' I projected my thoughts to him, not even trying to hide my anger. Brandon didn't know I was anything more than human, so I couldn't let him know that Lucius was anything more to me than a friend. However, as Justina's power was a Coven secret, I couldn't say it without permission. Lucius' brow furrowed but he nodded, covering his face with his hands.

"Justina is unique, even for a witch." I stated, breathing deeply, and Brandon and Chris looked at me strangely, waiting for me to continue. "She can cast both without a wand and silently."

"Mental casting?!" Chris exclaimed, both shocked and excited and a sharp look from me made him lower his voice. "But the implications of that are huge! Magic is shaped by the sound of a witches' voice and focused through their wands. To be able to cast without doing that would change everything we know about them and -"

"Would make them more dangerous." Brandon nodded, deep in thought. "Makes since that would be kept a secret. I'd imagine other witches would not welcome someone like that."

"No," I answered softly, "They don't, but for our suspect to know that, means they must've known Justina before she came to The Capital. Only those high in Command know within Lucius' Coven. Justina told me once before and now, everyone in this room knows."

I shot a glare at Chris and the sullen look on his face and his uncomfortable gulp made it clear that my point had gotten across.

"So, if his plan was to take Justina out so she couldn't cast without him knowing," LeAlexende spoke, his voice soft as he contributed to the conversation. "Doesn't that mean that he hasn't actually committed his crime yet?"

"Shit, he's right." Brandon cursed, "Which means he is choosing his Supernatural victims to some extent, he has to be if he knows what they're capable of. That supports the pixie theory, but god that's a lot of work for a bugger like that."

"I'll get the rest of the team on conference and we'll go through each of the previous victims again with this new outlook, maybe we can find something similar with the other killings before he tries to go for his actual kill." Brandon nodded to Chris and the agent turned to leave the waiting room. "You stay here and call me if she wakes up. Keep me updated on her progress. I don't want to press her if she makes it through but...if she knew someone who could do this, we could finally stop this lunatic."

"I know." I nodded and they walked back to the elevator, talking among themselves. Soon after my boss and coworker disappeared, Kisten appeared, pushing Justina's bed into the room with the other doctor. Kisten held the door open as they moved her into one of the rooms and closed the door as the other doctor went inside to finish getting her set up. As soon as we were alone, Lucius leapt to his feet, facing his old friend.

"Kis-"

"She's alive." We all sighed with relief at these words and waited for him to continue. Kisten pulled his gloves off his hands, refusing to look at any of us. "But it is bad. We did what we could, gave her a transfusion, but whoever it was, they were clearly attempting to kill her. She's unlikely to wake up for a few days."

"But she's alive and she'll survive?" Lucius asked cautiously, clearly preparing himself for a harsh response. Kisten sighed, running his hand through his dark hair. I wanted to hug him, to squeeze his hand and tell him he had done all that he could but knew how impossible that was. Lucius walked towards the Alpha, his voice soft. "Kisten?"

"It depends on her. She suffered no main organ damage and it seems like she's been casting a healing spell on herself unconsciously." Kisten admitted, dropping his hand back to his side. "We stitched up her large gashes and set her bones so that they heal properly but..."

"Wait, she had broken bones?" I interrupted, my tone incredulous, and Kisten nodded, giving me a strange look.

Yasmina Iro

"Yea, both of her legs were broken as well as…" I turned around to call my boss as Kisten watched me confused. I heard Lucius explaining to him about my case as my phone rang. Brandon could barely squeeze out a hello before I interrupted him.

"Put me on the call." I demanded and resumed as soon as I could hear the background noise of my other co-workers. "She has broken bones. Both legs."

"Broken bones? Well that kills the pixie theory." My female coworker, Julia, sounded disappointed. "I mean, a pixie killing a witch is ludicrous to begin with, but a cunning one could've pulled it off."

"Yea, but no pixie would have the inhuman strength needed to break a bone that quickly." Chris spoke, and it sounded like he was still writing on his notepad. I motioned for the two Overseers and Kisten to be silent and carefully put my phone on speaker. "Meaning there's really only two species who can both overcome a witch's spell and still possess inhuman strength to snap leg bones."

"Harpies and Dökkálfar, right?" Brandon offered and I noticed Kisten shook his head, holding up his index finger. I spoke quickly, looking at him confused.

"Actually, there's one more." Kisten scrambled to the waiting room table and began to draw something on one of the magazines. I could hear the disbelief of my colleagues as I waited to see what Kisten wanted to tell me.

"What? We ruled out gremlins and vila a long time ago and pixies just got ruled out." Another one of my teammates, Justin, spoke up. "If not harpies or Dökkálfar, then what?"

Kisten finally finished his drawing and the picture chilled me to my core. I knew what it was, but I was uncomfortable saying its name out loud, and I understood why he didn't want to either.

"An empousa." I whispered and the background noise grew deadly silent on both ends of the phone. No one dared breathe after I said the word out loud. Quietly, Chris started to whisper on his end with Brandon.

"But…aren't they extinct? I thought they were wiped out by… Mater Vitae a long time ago."

43 | P a g e

"Even with the tell of a copper limb, it would be hard to be sure of that." Justin reasoned. "It is completely possible that a few could've survived and are in hiding to avoid Hunters."

"But records of empousa are scarce, we barely know anything about them and even if we knew more, it's not like any would be registered in our system." Brandon sighed heavily, clearly not happy. "Dammit, every clue we get sets us back more. Raiven, ask Lucius if there is anything he could tell us about these empousa, including if he ever knew any. Meanwhile, we'll keep looking into any connections the other victims could have with Justina. Knowing the species is good and all but does us no good if we can't find the motive."

"Will do." I nodded and waited until he hung up before turning to Lucius. He had an unreadable look on his face and was looking away out the window. I moved to speak, but Kisten stopped me, shaking his head. He looked after Lucius with a painful look on his face and LeAlexende was also pensive.

"One of my former Retainers was an Empousa." Lucius breathed and a pit immediately formed in my stomach. "But she wouldn't have known about Justina. She...was hunted long before Justina came to us. Before I even crossed the sea."

"Plumeria was definitely killed, no question." Kisten added, crossing his arms. His tone was somber and regretful, as if he blamed himself for what happened. "We were there when the Hunters attacked her. We tried to protect her-"

"There were too many. They...almost killed us too." Lucius finished: the memory clearly painful for him as well. "Plumeria was such a kind soul, she was never much of a fighter. They overpowered her so easily-"

"Lucius." I stopped him, placing my hand on his shoulder. After a moment, he softly touched it, giving me a slight squeeze. "I'm sorry."

"It's alright, it was my own weakness that allowed Plumeria to be taken from me." Lucius' voice darkened as he continued. "We will not lose Justina to anyone."

"No, we won't." I agreed, stepping away. I turned back to face Kisten, who was still pensive. "I am more than a little concerned about our culprit being possibly an empousa. I won't say he doesn't have reason to want to attack other Supernaturals, but the Hunters wiped them out, not the community."

"Hunters were ordered by Mother to eradicate them, but they certainly had a lot of help from others." Kisten sighed, shaking his head as he took off his coat and I noticed the blood on his shirt. He must've started surgery before donning his coat: it was probably the other doctor who had forced him to wear it. He folded it over his arm as he continued. "Shapeshifters have always been treated poorly among Supernaturals: I'd imagine many of them were given up to the Hunters once Mother decided to eradicate them."

"But none of our victims have been known to work with Hunters, current or former." I remarked, and Kisten raised his eyebrows. I shrugged, folding my arms across my chest. "Just seemingly random, unless he's hunting those who are related to others who ratted out empousa to the Hunters."

"Then he would have no reason to be here." Lucius sneered, clearly upset. "No one turned Plumeria to them, we did our best to hide her copper hand from outsiders. Most of my current Command came after I crossed the sea. None of them would've known about Plumeria."

Kisten looked like he disagreed for a moment but said nothing. Lucius seemed not to notice and continued with his rant. "We were ambushed on our way back from visiting a friend and their target was clearly me. They didn't know she was an Empousa until she tried to defend me."

"It's okay, Lucius. We'll figure this out." I spoke softly as he turned to face me, his expression still blank. "This is what I do. We didn't have a chance to prevent the other killings, but we won't allow him to kill on our own turf. This is as personal to my team as it is to us, trust me on that."

"I do." He stated plainly, and LeAlexende sighed, finally turning our attention to him. He had remained silent during most of our exchange and I had forgotten he was with us. Lucius' expression changed, smiling wryly. "I'm sorry Alexende, but I must ask that you shorten your visit."

"Unnecessary, I'm here to help." LeAlexende's tone was strange as he turned to look at me. "Raiven, can you tell me where and when all the other killings occurred? I have connections to determine if an empousa was present in any of those areas."

"Connections?" I queried and he nodded, refusing to say more. I was suspicious but Lucius nodded and gave me a silent order. I knew better than to argue and merely turned to Kisten. "Do you have anywhere I can get actual paper?"

"Yea, follow me." As I followed Kisten out of the waiting room, I could hear the two friends whispering behind us.

6

"What do you make of this, Kisten?" I leaned back in his chair as I finished writing down the list LeAlexende had asked for. Kisten had taken me to his office, which was down the hallway from Justina's room. The office was pristine and immaculate, not a single paper or pen out of place. It reflected the personality that Kisten projected so perfectly: calm, clean and under control.

Kisten remained quiet and seemed to be deep in thought. He had barely moved as I finished writing my list, staring at one of the many charts in his office. I sighed at his lack of a response, allowing myself to spring forward in the office chair.

"That something still isn't right." He spoke, shaking his head and surprising me. "It's too convenient. Empousas were hunted several centuries ago, so if your suspect was an empousa, why wait until now? And why include humans at all, why not just kill individual Supernaturals? Why kill so many if they aren't the target?"

"I know, and you're not wrong. That's been the whole problem with this case." I closed my eyes, thinking of the previous crime scene. A high school gym, the scene of a prom gone horribly wrong. I still remembered walking into the side room where the murders took place and a shiver ran through me. "Some of the victims are too young to have been involved at all with the Hunters."

"Then it seems unlikely it would be an empousa."

"I know, but then why?" I leaned forward on his desk, cradling my head. "It's been my biggest headache. There's no obvious motive, nothing that strings all these victims together. Brandon said it best: the more we learn, the less this all makes sense. Every new crime kills any previous theory."

"So, an empousa is your best lead." Kisten leaned against his desk and I stood, touching his arm. He absently placed his hand on mine, sighing again. "I don't like this. It feels like we're missing the writing on the wall."

"I know." I stepped closer to him, releasing his arm, and reaching for his face. He instinctively stopped me, grabbing my wrist without even looking up to me. I grunted, annoyed by his reaction and he sighed heavily.

"You know you can't." He closed his eyes, refusing to look at me. His grip on my hand tightened for a moment. "I can't keep giving in to-"

"Please." I pleaded, and Kisten looked up to see my face. As our eyes met, I could finally see just how hard this was on him and Kisten's worry for both Justina and Lucius was plain on his face. He once told me that Lucius was like a quiet beehive: if you left it alone and didn't try to knock it over, everything was fine. However, the moment a member of the colony was hurt, the whole swarm would never leave you alone until you paid for your crime.

Kisten slowly released my hand, and I softly touched his face, at first only allowing my fingertips to touch his skin. Even with such a soft gesture, Kisten purred slightly and leaned into my hand, clearly showing how much he craved my touch. My chest ached at the sight of my skin against his: the contrast of my dark skin against his tan complexion always made my heart skip a beat.

Taking a deep breath, I placed my whole hand against his cheek and as he sighed his contentment, I hissed with pain. My whole hand felt like it was burning and the longer I held my hand to his face, the more my body screamed with pain. It traveled down my arm and I pulled it away as the heat reached my chest. I held my aching arm and Kisten quickly grabbed my shoulder, causing me to wince. He loosened his grip, lightly stroking my short sleeve.

"Are you alright? It didn't hurt too badly?" I shook my head as I forced a smile, releasing my still aching arm. He looked at me with concern and my heart began pounding in my chest.

"I'm fine, Kisten. I just wanted to give you some comfort." I smiled as I looked into his eyes and I reached up to touch his face again. This time he grabbed my arm, stopping me long before I reached his face.

"Don't tempt me like this, Raiven." He pleaded, his voice high-pitched as he closed his eyes. My heart pounded from his words, but I remained silent. He slowly opened his eyes, turning his gloomy gaze to me. "I don't want to hurt you."

"You're not, the Oath is." I scoffed, pulling my arm away and Kisten looked as if he wanted to reach for me, but he stopped himself. I reached for him instead, hugging him tightly as I kept my arms on his shirt. He grew still under my touch before gently wrapping his arms around me, careful not to touch my skin. I dropped my head into his chest, sighing heavily with my frustration. "It isn't your fault and I would never blame you."

"It is my fault." Kisten leaned down, careful to lay his head on my shoulder and to avoid touching my neck. This was as intimate as he would allow us to get and the most he had touched me in more than a year. Anymore, and the Oath of Loyalty would ensure that I would pay the price. "I should've had Lucius release me from the Oath a long time ago."

"Why didn't you?" I asked tentatively, my voice soft and quiet. Kisten grew still again, and I regretted my question. We remained in silence for a long time, holding each other. I tightened my grip around him and after a moment, he sighed, returning my gesture.

"It didn't matter to me at the time." He spoke softly and slowly, his breath warm against my skin. I felt my heart pound, moving into my throat as he leaned into me more, almost standing from his desk. "I...never thought I'd find someone else I wanted like this."

"You mean you've never been with anyone?" I pushed him back, looking at him incredulously. He looked away from me, slightly blushing. I couldn't help the accusing smile that started on my face. "Kisten, you're three hundred years old, and you're telling me you've never been with anyone?"

"It's not like I never wanted too." He retorted, still blushing. I couldn't help a small giggle at his reaction. It faded when he turned to face me, his eyes filled with loss. "I just...couldn't ever be with them and I ...gave up when they finally died. I felt like I had died."

"I-I'm sorry Kisten." I started to pull away from him, but he kept his arms wrapped around me, still careful not to touch my skin. I could feel his breath against my face and for a moment, I thought he was going to kiss me and despite how painful I knew it would be, my heart pounded at the thought. Instead, I felt him dig his hands into my side, pulling at the fabric of my shirt.

"Don't be." He whispered, his breath hot and heavy as he breathed his words against my skin, allowing his breath to caress me. His hands gripped me more tightly through my clothing and I was slightly surprised by his actions. Kisten always maintained an incredibly careful and calm demeanor, always distancing himself from me when he thought he was losing control. He growled softly, his voice sounding animalistic. "You're all that I want now."

A sudden knock at his door made him release me, and we quickly pulled away from each other. Kisten closed his eyes for a moment as I tried to smooth out my shirt. The shifter adjusted himself, settling into a more comfortable position against his desk.

"Come in." He called out and the door opened to LeAlexende, who quietly stepped into the office. The Overseer had a solemn expression, still perturbed by what he had witnessed at the Coven. He closed the door slowly, still lost in thought as he looked at the floor.

"Is your list ready?" He looked up, and from the look he gave each of us, it was clear he suspected something. Clearing my throat, I reached to the desk and handed him the paper.

"Yes, it is. All the known killings that have been attributed to our suspect and their locations." I said as he glanced it over, nodding as he folded it. "I hope it's useful."

"Me too. I'll start using it as soon as I get settled in Justina's room." Kisten nodded solemnly at the Overseer's words. "Lucius has asked that I remain to watch her while I reach out to my contacts. I will give both of you a call if and when her condition changes."

"Thank you, LeAlexende. For everything." Kisten dropped to his knee as he bowed to the Overseer, and after a moment, I followed. Le Alexende merely smiled as he stood us up, his expression somewhat like his previous cheery nature.

"You and Lucius are good friends of mine. This is just as personal to me as it is to you." I gave Kisten a questioning look as the Overseer turned to leave. LeAlexende paused in the doorway, barely glancing over his shoulder to talk to us. "Oh, by the way, Lucius wants all of Command in pairs from now on. You two are to stay together at all times, or at least until the culprit is caught."

Both Kisten and I stood shocked as LeAlexende made his way out, closing the door behind him. My heart was pounding as I stared at the closed door, my mind still trying to process what I had heard. Slowly, we turned to look at each other before Kisten bolted to his door, walking out of it with me shortly behind. We caught Lucius just as Eve walked out of the elevator into the waiting room.

"Lucius." Kisten called his name plainly, and Lucius turned to face us as Eve settled herself in his lap. Eve shot both of us an angry glance before snuggling up to Lucius and as usual, her display made me want to gag. Kisten ignored Eve entirely as he continued speaking. "Why am I paired with Raiven? Wouldn't it make more sense for me to be with you? Or even Eve?"

"Eve will be with me." Lucius stated matter-of-factly, wrapping his arm around his Retainer. It wasn't uncommon for Overseers to be romantically involved with their Retainer or Alpha or both in some cases. Most of Command disapproved of her being Retainer, since most of us felt her power-hungry nature made her unfit to fill the role. Ultimately, we had no choice but to accept Lucius' decision until she died, or he replaced her. "There isn't anyone else I can pair you with. Liel and Crispin are paired, and I have Aurel with Grace. Yoreile, I have him paired with Quinn. Everyone else is out of the area."

"Problem, Kisten?" Eve asked innocently and Kisten glared at her. Eve went out of her way to try and make Kisten miserable, jealous of his long friendship with Lucius. She lacked the understanding that the two weren't involved romantically in any way and continued to perceive him as a rival. Like her jealousy of me, Eve was excellent at overlooking the obvious if she felt someone was standing in her way. "I didn't think you had anything against her."

"I don't, but-" Kisten stopped himself, holding his head in his hands as I remained silent. I understood why he didn't want to be paired with me: Kisten had spent the better part of a year keeping me at arm's length, making sure he wouldn't lose his precious control. He took a deep breath as he chose his next words. "I'm not allowed at the Coven: I was only stopping by today because you asked me to prepare dinner. The Rules still require Raiven to stay."

"The Rules don't bind Raiven the same way." Lucius spoke nonchalantly, Eve leaning her head against his shoulder. "That's why she can be paired with you. She'll just have to stay at your house."

My heart was pounding so loud I could barely hear Kisten as he continued to try and find a way to get out of me staying with him. Stuck at his house, always required to be in the same space as him: it sounded like torture of the cruelest kind. I could barely stand being alone with him for a few hours before I wanted to strip him of his clothing, much less days. Kisten certainly knew this as he continued to argue until Lucius stopped him.

"I've made my decision, Kisten." Lucius narrowed his blue eyes, his hair slightly standing on end as he grew annoyed. "Despite my faith in your and Raiven's power, I will not risk having either of you alone. Now unless you can give me a *valid* reason as to why you cannot be with Raiven, this conversation is over."

Kisten stopped, seeing he could not talk Lucius out of this without telling the truth. He stood still for a moment, and I held my breath, waiting to see what he would do. Finally, he dropped his shoulders, taking a deep breath before turning to face me.

"I'll be right back, then we can go." He muttered, walking past me back down to his office. I was slightly surprised that he wasn't honest: I'd imagine if Eve hadn't been there, he might have been. I was torn between whether I was supposed to follow him or stay when Lucius called my name.

"Raiven, please." I turned to face him, his cool eyes on me as he stroked Eve's side, my heart aching as I watched. When he spoke again, I forced myself to look away from his hand and to his face. "Take care of him. He won't admit it, but he's not as happy being alone as he says."

'*Don't I know it.*' I merely nodded as Kisten returned and walked past me without saying a word. I gave Lucius one final glance as I hurried after him, barely making it to the elevator before it closed.

7

I silently stared out the window as we drove out of Decver, watching the sky as the sun set beyond the horizon. Kisten was silent as well and kept his eyes on the road, refusing to look at me. I knew he was thinking the same thing as me: how long we could deal with this before we both went insane.

My desire for Kisten had been purely physical when we first met. He simply was attractive to me: dark hair, mysterious eyes, and longevity to boot. After he told me that he was still bound to Lucius and Eve via the Oath, I had tried to just be his friend after seeing how miserable he was. Kisten always kept to himself unless he was needed and didn't really go anywhere for fun.

The more time we had spent trying to be friends however, the more I started to fall for him. Underneath all that careful control was a man who wanted to let go and enjoy life and I felt special that he allowed me to be a part of that. However, after realizing how badly the Oath could hurt me, Kisten started avoiding me, only interacting with me when he had too.

It made sense why Lucius would pair us: as far as he knew, we were still friends and he had always approved of my friendship with Kisten. It sometimes seemed as if he was trying to push us into a relationship, with the way he set up some of our hangouts. He had been surprised when we suddenly stopped and I merely told him that Kisten wanted some space, leaving it at that.

He was also right about the Rules: other than Kisca, who was a pixie, I was the only other member of Command who could ignore the Rules. Mater Vitae had made the Rules before creating us, so we were only as bound to them as we wanted to be. If she wanted too, Mater Vitae probably could've fixed that problem with the system, but as many of us hated or feared her too much to work with her by time she found out, I doubt she cared anymore.

"I don't have much at home." Kisten suddenly spoke, his hands gripping the wheel tightly as his words pulled me from my thoughts. I only continued to watch him in the window's reflection and didn't turn to look at his face. He glanced at me before returning his attention to the road, his tone tentative. "Raiven?"

"I heard you." I sighed, closing my eyes. "You know I don't care. You never have much at home."

"Okay." He stopped talking and returned his attention to driving. We sat in silence for a moment longer before he spoke again, his voice barely above a whisper. "Are you gonna be okay with this?"

"I'm much more worried about you." I admitted, leaning back in my seat as I laid it all the way back. I opened my eyes to stare at the roof of the car, frowning slightly. "You're the one who started avoiding me, remember?"

"It's not like I wanted to. But the Oath..." his voice trailed off as he considered his next words. When he spoke again, his voice was quiet as he took his exit off the highway, leaning back as he stopped at the light. "It's not like I didn't miss you."

"I missed you too." I admitted, my heart aching as the light changed. I paused, watching the trees fly by the window as we drove closer to his residence. My voice was soft when I spoke again, filled with my longing. "Every time I have to see other people being happy together, I miss you."

"At least I wasn't the only one." He laughed slightly, moving his hand to touch my leg. Halfway through the movement, it was almost as if he realized what he was doing and he stopped himself, his hand hovering awkwardly. I looked down as he pulled his hand back to the wheel, clearing his throat. It was another long moment before he spoke, turning into his neighborhood. "I just don't want to hurt you, Raiven."

"Like I said earlier, you never have. That's all the Oath's doing, and well," I paused as he pulled into his driveway, backing his car into the garage as it opened. "If you want to be technical, we both know whose fault that is."

"Mater Vitae?"

"Her too." I let my seat up and unbuckled myself as he turned off the car. Deep in my mind, I blamed Mother for everything that happened and most Supernaturals did. She created us, bound us with all these Rules and Oaths, and then placed us in a society where, until recently, we were hated, feared, and killed. Now as far as most of us knew, she was hidden, protected by her loyal Hunters. Fairies were her last creation before most of us denounced her and shortly after, she retreated, although no one knows why or where. I had my own suspicions as to why, but no one knew for sure why she gave up.

Kisten unlocked his door and bolted inside his house as I took my time noticing the changes he had made to the garage. I hadn't been in his house during the past year and unsurprisingly, there were hardly any changes. Ever since arriving in the Americas, Kisten only occasionally updated his home and hadn't moved from this plot of land since him and Lucius arrived in The Capital back in 1834. He had the garage added shortly before I came to Decver, and only did so because of the city complaining about the state of his driveway.

As such, the inside of his house always had an air of nostalgia and I breathed it in as I stepped inside. Kisten was busy closing his curtains and turning on lights, clearly not expecting to have been gone all afternoon. I leaned in the doorway, watching him as he moved about, starting to notice certain changes about him. Kisten's hair was slightly longer than usual, as it was starting to reach his shoulders. He also seemed to have gained a little weight, filling out his shirt a little better than I remembered. While an amazing cook, Kisten only ate enough to stay alive and rarely ate for pleasure, meaning his weight gain was probably muscle.

"Uh, Raiven?" I shook my head as Kisten moved in front of me, a worried look on his face. I looked up to him, slightly embarrassed.

"Huh?"

"I asked if you were hungry." He leaned down close to me, taking in my scent. His eyes shined when he pulled back to look at me again. "You don't smell like you've eaten today."

"You know I don't like it when you do that." I huffed, walking past him to the couch. Kisten chuckled as he walked into the kitchen, examining what little food he had. He pulled out some ingredients as I turned on his TV, turning to some cartoons. I was barely paying attention, however, my mind returning to Justina as I removed my shoes. I couldn't shake that I knew for certain what could cause wounds like that and the answer was evading me. I closed my eyes as I laid down, seeing Justina's wounded body as I held her in my lap. Large gashes as if ripped open by claws, but somehow all avoiding vital areas. Was Justina attempting to defend herself and that's why they broke her legs?

"Why not just kill her, though?" I wondered out loud, looking up to the roof. Witches weren't difficult to kill: their lifespans were only slightly longer than humans and besides their use of magic, anything that could kill a human would kill a witch. "To torture her? But why? No one else was-"

"Food's ready." The delicious smell wafted towards me as I sat up, looking toward Kisten in the kitchen. He was portioning food on a plate as I wandered up to him and sat at his breakfast bar. He slid a plate with the appetizing food in front of me: it was some sort of chicken and pasta and one bite confirmed my suspicions. My hunger consumed me and I wolfed down the food with all the vigor of a starving animal. Kisten laughed as he watched, leaning on the counter.

"There's more if you want." He nodded to the skillet and I paused in my eating, slurping up a noodle.

"You aren't going to eat?"

"Not hungry. I hunted yesterday." Kisten tapped his hand on the counter, smiling at me. Kisten's nearest neighbor was miles away and a decent stretch of woods separated them. Sometimes Kisten would hunt in the woods, helping himself to any prey he could find. He said it helped to keep his animal in check, and he encouraged all of his pack to do so, allowing them to come over whenever they wanted to indulge their animal. Sometimes he would go with the newbies to help them, but he often let them figure it out for themselves.

"You're a good Alpha." I commented, smiling as I took my time finishing my food. His smile broadened slightly at that, reaching for my free hand. I let him take it and winced as he started stroking the back of my hand, the skin burning slightly. Kisten must've noticed as he quickly released me, standing up from the counter.

"I'll be right ba-"

"Don't go." I choked out, trying to swallow my food so I could stop him. He paused in his movement, leaning against the counter on the opposite side of the kitchen. He looked away from me, not meeting my gaze as I coughed to clear my throat of food. "It didn't hurt that much. Just unexpected. Usually touching my hands doesn't hurt."

"Intentions matter." Kisten sighed, running his hand through his hair. "Whether I want to be intimate matters."

"Want to be..." I let the sentence trail, keeping my eyes on Kisten as I finished eating. He still was refusing to look at me, keeping his eyes to the floor. He had started to unbutton his shirt while cooking and I could see the hair on his chest, lighter in color than the dark brown waves that graced his crown. Kisten looked so majestic in his simple dress clothes, hiding the passion I knew he kept under lock and key. I finished my food, continuing to undress him with my eyes.

"You want to be intimate, huh?" I purred, standing up as I carried my empty plate into the kitchen. I reached around him to drop the dish into the sink, sliding my bandaged hand around his waist.

"Raiven..." Kisten looked at me as if he feared my intentions, and I smiled, wrapping my other arm around him. Kisten seemed torn between returning my gesture and pulling away before finally settling on lightly touching my shoulders, careful to stay on clothing. I gripped his shirt tighter, pressing myself into him. I earned myself a soft gasp of surprise and I smiled coyly, looking up to his face.

"Yes, Kisten?" I asked, pressing my body more into his as several expressions pass through his beautiful features. As much as I found Kisten's control attractive, I wanted him to let go. I wanted to see the passion he had only let me experience sparingly, just enough to make me want more.

"Raiven, don't do this." he pleaded, his hands digging into my shoulders as he fought himself. I smiled, burying my face into his chest, and ignoring his plea. I pressed my leg between his, and I could feel him as he started to become aroused. He was looking for a way to escape me, but his own desire betrayed him as he kept his grip on my shoulders. My own desire began to grow as I slid my hands up his back and dug my fingers into his skin.

He gasped at the movement and without thinking, he grabbed my chin and slid his mouth across mine. My lips and mouth exploded with fire as he kissed me deeply, forcing his tongue into my mouth. Despite the pain, I felt heat growing in another part of my body and I returned the gesture, sliding my tongue against his as the scalding heat consumed my face. It was as if my flesh would burst into flames if the kiss continued, but Kisten pulled back, panting heavily. I also panted, touching my lips as the heat began to fade.

"Are you alright?"

"Yea," I smiled, wincing slightly as I dropped my hand back to his waist. Kisten had a dark look on his face, his chartreuse eyes swirling. His devilish expression reminded me more of Crispin, but on him, it only excited me. Kisten moved his hands from my shoulder to my waist, a smirk on his face.

"Good." With this, he kissed me again and I moaned with both pain and desire. It felt as if he were literally setting me on fire with his touch and it excited me as much as it hurt. I could feel his fingers as he fumbled at my shirt and searing pain followed his hand as he touched my back. I merely clung to him as he stroked me, indulging in his own desires.

It was clear his control was fading as Kisten pulled back again, his fangs visible in his mouth as he panted. I took this moment to free myself of him, leaning against the breakfast bar across from him. Kisten made as if to follow me, but gripped the sink behind him, attempting to restrain himself. Both of us were panting as we watched the other, and I smiled, despite the ache left from his touch and kiss.

"Gods, Kisten, keep this up and you'll make me a masochist." I breathed, my smile broadening. Kisten merely growled in response, and I felt a clench in my lower regions. We had barely been alone together an hour, and this is where we were, panting on opposite sides of his kitchen as he tried his best to not strip me of my clothing and take me on his counter. Neither of us were sure if the Oath would kill me or make me wish I was dead, but I had stopped caring about that more than a year ago.

"Raiven, I can smell you." Kisten growled, almost as if he were in pain. I grew worried as I saw fur start to sprout on his arms and quickly recede into his skin. I couldn't fathom that Kisten was losing control of his animal: he was far too experienced to lose control like this. "I can smell how wet you are, and it makes me want you more."

I shifted uncomfortably as he said this, looking away and trying to calm myself down. I hated when Kisten mentioned my own scents to me: it always made me feel dirty and transparent. Kisten laughed darkly at my attempts to calm down and I turned away from him completely, facing the breakfast bar. This turned out to be a mistake as I soon saw Kisten's hands on the counter next to mine, and he pressed himself into me, now fully aroused and making me aware of it. I didn't try to hide my moan as he grinded against me, leaning down to breathe in my scent.

"My animal wants you." He growled into my ear, and I couldn't help but shudder against him. He lightly dragged his teeth against my skin, careful to avoid scratching me with his fangs and his spots lightly appeared on his hands, despite the lack of fur. Smelling my desire, my lust for him was finally sending his animal over the edge, and probably for the first time in a long time, he was losing control. "I want you."

"Now who's not being fair Kisten?" I moaned halfheartedly, doing my best to not push myself against him. Kisten, however, did not care for my restraint and grabbed my hips, thrusting me into the counter. I moaned loudly, dragging my nails against the marble. The shifter behind me repeated his action, loosely grabbing my neck and lifting my head up. He slid his other hand down the front of my body, pressing into my stomach.

"I don't care anymore. I haven't cared for a long time." He whispered darkly into my ear, and even through our clothing, I could feel his arousal throbbing, and it caused me to clench in response. His burning grip on my throat tightened for a moment, and Kisten growled into my skin. "I know you don't either."

He reached under my shirt again, sliding his free hand up to my breasts. Even through the bra, intense heat danced across my skin as he fondled me and he growled, kissing my neck as he played with me. His nails began growing into claws and I gave into my moans, not even trying to hide my pleasure from him. This is what I had wanted: for Kisten to give into me, to give into his desires...

I opened my eyes, having a moment of clarity despite the pain and pleasure. This wasn't Kisten giving in to himself: this was him giving into his animal and I knew that Kisten would regret it if it went much further. I did my best to hold back my moans and fought to find my voice.

"You're right, I don't." I breathed, trying to do everything to not focus on his breath on my neck and his member throbbing against my back. "But I also don't want you to regret loving me tomorrow."

Kisten stiffened for a moment, his hands relaxing their grip before he released me all together. His hands reappeared on the counter and it was clear he was trying to reign in the beast. His hands slowly shifted back to being human, and his spots faded, but remained slightly visible on his skin. His throbbing member in my back betrayed where his desires lay but he was at least trying to regain control of his lust.

Hesitantly, I leaned back against him and he did his best to hold me gently this time, wrapping his arms around my middle. He took in a deep breath and released it shakily, burying his face into my short afro. I considered pulling away from him, but instead, I gently touched his arm, before carefully resting my arms on his, my skin burning where we touched.

"You're right. I would regret it." Kisten spoke, his voice still containing a slight growl. "I...wouldn't want my first time with you to be like this, with my animal controlling me."

"I won't say it's not hot though." I laughed softly and he chuckled, the sound vibrating in his chest behind me. "Something different."

"You don't have to tell me that." He postured, nibbling on my ear and causing a slight burning sensation there. He leaned down again, licking my earlobe before whispering into it. "I can still smell how much you want me."

"Kisten." I whined, closing my eyes in embarrassment. He laughed again, pressing kisses into the back of my neck, each one a burning sensation of pleasure and pain.

"You say you hate it, but I love it. I love knowing exactly how much you want me." He spoke in between his kisses, slowly sliding one of his hands under my shirt again. The pain that seared across my middle section almost outweighed the pleasurable sensation, but just knowing that he was touching me, that it was Kisten's hand on my skin made me love the feeling. "How much the pain isn't bothering you. Should've told me how much you loved it."

"I think someone is turning into a sadist." I teased, reaching my bandaged hand up to stroke his face, my fingers burning as they touched his skin. He removed his hand from under my shirt and I was both disappointed and relieved. Suddenly, I was lifted into the air and I reached to grab Kisten as he lifted me up and walked towards his couch. He turned off the television and climbed on top of me, settling between my legs. I fully expected him to drop on top of me, but he remained on his knees, keeping my legs spread with his hands. I reached up to him, laying my hands on his. "Where was this lack of control a year ago?"

"This is your fault. All your teasing touches, always wanting me, despite me doing my best to stay away. It was only a matter of time before you would win." His eyes swirled again, and I could still see his fangs as he smiled a toothy smile. He lifted my leg to his shoulder, kissing my thigh through the pants. "I could smell it every time, Raiven and it always took so much to walk away. Even now, it's taking all my control not to just take you."

"You call this restraint?" I pulled my hands back, placing them under my head as Kisten laughed again. He laid another kiss on my pants, squeezing my thigh tightly. He leaned down, letting my leg rest on his shoulder as he slid his hands toward my waist.

"I call it compromise." With this, Kisten leaned over, carefully reaching to undo my pants and release me from them. I couldn't help but tense up slightly, but Kisten lightly kissed my exposed thigh before removing the offensive clothing entirely. "Don't worry, I won't undress you more than this."

Before I could question him, I found my lower half being lifted up and Kisten had his face buried in between my legs, breathing in my scent as his hands were carefully placed on my underwear. I couldn't help but be embarrassed as he breathed me in, and I covered my face as he sighed contently. A long, wet lick told me of his intentions, and I moaned slightly, peeking through my arms to look up at him. He had his eyes closed, licking me through my panties and enjoying both my taste and scent. I still could experience small flashes of heat despite the clothing separating his tongue from me but these small flashes only added to my pleasure. I moaned freely as Kisten enjoyed his treat, keeping my underwear between us as he indulged himself as much as he dared. Finally, he paused, laying a burning kiss on my thigh.

"I could eat you all day. My delicious chocolate angel..." He breathed, taking another long lick and I moaned openly, frustrated by the underwear. Despite the intense pain it would bring, I wanted to feel his mouth against me, to feel his tongue as he tasted me deeply. Kisten must've seen the desire on my face, as he carefully pulled my underwear aside, soaked from both my juices and his saliva. He paused, taking in the view and embarrassment started creeping in again.

"Beautiful." He whispered, leaning into me and I closed my eyes in anticipation. No amount of warning could've prepared me for the searing pain: the second his tongue touched me, pain shot through my whole body, like a painful orgasm. It flooded all my nerves, but on the edge of the pain was pleasure, sweet pleasure as each lick of his sandpaper tongue sent another wave through my body. He thrusted his tongue into me and I couldn't stay silent anymore.

"Kisten!" my voice was somewhere between a moan and a scream as I cried out. Kisten immediately stopped and dropped me down, moving my arms to see my face.

"Raiven?! Raiven, are you alright?" His voice was full of concern, and I had to take a couple of breaths to calm myself down enough to open my eyes. I could see his mouth, damp with my juices and I tried to smile, forcing my aching body up. I supported myself with one arm as I licked his face, tasting myself on his skin. He sighed with relief, hugging me loosely.

"It was painful," I admitted, and he stiffened again, but another lick from me relaxed him. "Probably the most pain I've been in for a long time, but it also felt so amazing."

"Imagine if I was inside of you." Kisten's voice dropped again, and I couldn't help but shudder as I imagined both the intense pleasure and pain that would cause.

"I'm not sure I could survive that." I breathed, laying back down and Kisten let me, gently kissing my stomach through my shirt. "As much as I would love it."

"I know." Kisten smiled, and he sat up again, this time using his hand to tease me. I moaned softly and his smile widened. "I'll do my best not to hurt you so much again. Just let me pleasure you this time."

He shifted my position so that he could still taste me while I laid down and I closed my eyes, drowning in the intense pleasure and soft pain as Kisten played with me as much as he dared.

To Catch A Raven

8

I woke up the next morning, not sure where I was as sunlight streamed on my face. Something on the bed shifted and I recognized the dark brown hair that graced the pillow next to me. I smiled, passing his hair between my fingers and pressing my face into him, my body still aching from the torture it had been submitted to.

"That tickles, Raiven." Kisten mumbled, shifting on the bed. I giggled, releasing him as I realized I was wearing a dark red shirt and underwear, different from the blue I had passed out wearing.

"Not my fault you have beautiful hair." I sat up, looking around for my clothing and my pants. A frown started on my face as I failed to find them, and I shook Kisten gently. "Kisten, what did you do with my clothes?"

"They're in the hamper." He yawned, stretching out like a cat on the bed and his toes curling as the sheet shifted down. He opened his eyes and pointed to the small hamper that was overflowing with dirty clothes. "I didn't want to leave you in soiled clothing, so I managed to find some clothes you had left here."

"Okay what about my pants?" Kisten groaned as he motioned towards a chair in the corner, my pants laid neatly across it. I fell back down, yawning loudly as I tried to finish waking up. He was shirtless but was still wearing pants as he laid next to me. I didn't remember him ever taking off his shirt, but from the lingering sensation on my arms, I had a suspicion that he had fallen asleep cuddling me.

I kissed his hair again as I stood out of the bed, surprised by how refreshed my body seemed. My body felt looser and more limber, despite the ache from the pain. I stretched toward the roof, curling my fingers in the air.

"What's the plan for today?" I turned around at hearing Kisten's voice and he was laying on the pillow, watching me as I stretched. I looked away, considering my plan of action for the day. I wanted to search for Justina's assaulter, but I still didn't have much information to go on. There wasn't much I could do without visiting the office but having to take Kisten with me would cause too many questions that I didn't want to have to answer.

"I haven't decided." I admitted, sitting back down on the bed, and Kisten shifted behind me, his arms appearing around my stomach. I hummed happily, stroking his arm. "I'm tempted to go to the Coven to check out Justina's room and see the scene for myself. But I can't exactly take you to the office with me."

"Well, I'm supposed to go visit one of the newbies who's having trouble shifting. A wolf pup: his parents are asking for help." He sighed, echoing my hum of contentment. "We could swing by the Coven, then you could join me in helping the pup, and after that we can go to the hospital. I need to check in on Justina and remove your stitches."

"Sounds good." A faint kiss on my back and I felt the bed move as Kisten stood up and moved to his closet to dress. He peeled off his dress pants and changed into a pair of jeans and a plain green t-shirt. I was surprised Kisten owned such clothing: I had never seen him wear anything so plain before. I slowly stood up and slipped on my own pants as Kisten slid on a simple pair of boots. I glanced around for my shoes, remembering I had taken them off next to the couch.

I started out of Kisten's room when a strong hand grabbed my arm and pulled me against him. He was standing in front of his mirror and looking at us together, holding me tightly against him. Kisten's eyes were looking at me lovingly, and he gently buried his face in my neck, sighing happily.

I couldn't help but smile, and I sighed as well, loving the feel of his arms around me. My thoughts turned to the previous night, and I couldn't help the clench in my middle as I remember the torture Kisten had subjected me too. The man in question looked up, his eyes darkening as he caught the change in my scent.

"Someone is thinking dirty thoughts." He whispered darkly, his eyes still locked with mine through the glass as he grinned. I cleared my throat and freed myself from his embrace. He allowed me, his hands lingering as I slid from him.

"Maybe we should go before we're stuck in this house all day." I escaped down the stairs and could hear Kisten's laugh behind me as he followed, his foot heavy on each step. Somehow, hearing his slow steps down the stairs only served to arouse me more and I almost ran into the living room to try to escape my own thoughts.

"You make it sound like you don't want that." His deepening voice followed me down the stairs as I sat on his couch to slide on my boots. Kisten walked into the kitchen, retrieving his keys from the counter. I stood to him standing over me, and he stole a kiss, burning my lips with his indulgence. "Your body says otherwise."

"Don't we have somewhere to be?" I tried to escape him, walking around the couch away from him, but Kisten stopped me, pinning me against the back of the couch. I leaned back as he leaned into me, chuckling. "Kisten, c'mon."

"What? Aren't you the one who started this last night?" he laughed, leaning down and breathing against my neck. There was no sign of his spots or fangs, so this was him acting without the influence of his animal. Kisten's eyes burned and I had to fight the smile that wanted to creep on my face. "Not up for finishing what you started?"

"I thought you did that." I pouted, closing my eyes as he licked my neck. The trail of fire left by his tongue was starting to excite me and I did my best to ignore the heat growing elsewhere in my body.

"I finished what *I* started." He corrected me, taking my hand and pressing it to his groin, allowing me to feel his throbbing member beneath the fabric. I inhaled sharply and I couldn't help but stroke him and earn myself a soft moan. "You, however, still have a debt."

I said nothing to this, unbuttoning his jeans and sliding my hand inside, stroking him through his sheer boxers. He gasped for me, gripping the couch with one hand and wrapping his other hand around my waist. I continued stroking him, teasing his head with my thumb, my fingertips on fire as I touched him. His moans and hot breath excited me more, and I could feel him starting to leak through his silk underwear.

I slowly knelt and pressed my face to him, taking in his scent. He was right: there was something arousing, exciting about being able to tell how much he wanted me. I kissed his arousal gently, my lips burning even with the fabric between us and he moaned above me. I looked up to see him looking down, his lips parted as he breathed. His eyes were swirling again, and I could see his fangs starting to grow in his mouth.

I stood back up, cradling his face in my hands. My unbandaged hand burned more than usual as I kissed him deeply, burning my mouth and tongue as I indulged myself. His sandpaper tongue added another layer of pain to the fire, but I was lost in the kiss.

"Let's continue this tonight." I breathed, trying to be a voice of reason in the madness of our passion as I pulled away. Kisten growled in response, and I stroked his cheek, my wrists growing weak from the pain. "My body needs time to recover Kisten. I promise I'll pleasure you this time."

Kisten considered my words, closing his eyes and standing away from me. He carefully redid his jeans, adjusting his erection to zip his pants. By the time he reopened his eyes, they were back to normal and he smiled softly. His grin still held darker things as he turned away from me, jingling his keys in his hand.

I followed the Alpha into the garage as he unlocked the doors and I slid quietly into the passenger seat. Kisten also climbed in without making a sound and started up his car, the electric engine practically silent compared to my noisy guzzler.

I watched the scenery fly past us as he drove us back into the city, but this time my thoughts were heavy with fear. I hadn't seen the true extent of Justina's injuries yet, and I was worried what the scene would look like for her to be injured so badly. My thoughts were in such turmoil that I barely noticed as Kisten pulled into the parking lot behind The Dream and was only brought to the present when the shifter lightly touched my shoulder.

"We're here." He offered and I slowly climbed out of the car, my hand lingering on the door as I looked toward the Coven's entrance. I closed the car door and began to walk to the simple entrance, each footstep heavy as I forced myself forward. I threw the door open, the sound of it banging the wall reminding me of Aurel's anger the day before. I looked down into the encroaching darkness and I paused, unsure in my movements.

"Are you okay, Raiven?" Once again, Kisten's voice drew me from my thoughts and I glanced back towards him. He was leaning against his car, a worried expression on his face and he pushed himself away from the vehicle as he walked towards me. I took a deep breath, turning to face the dark Coven stairs once again.

"I'm fine." I insisted, climbing down the dark stairwell as my eyes slowly adjusted. The hallway grew darker as Kisten closed the door behind us and I reached the last step, making my way to Justina's room. I could see the outlines of Quinn and Yoreile as they stood guard over the scene. Lucius took protecting crime scenes very seriously, and I wasn't surprised that he was treating this case no differently.

"It's just me." I announced my presence as I saw Quinn tense, the warlock's hands glowing as he summoned his power. Upon recognizing me, he dropped his hands, giving me a tired smile. Yoreile remained silent, not turning as Kisten and I approached. "I'm here to see the scene."

"Go ahead." Quinn conceded, stepping aside to allow me to enter as he released his power. I slowly pushed the door open and had to immediately cover my mouth from the display. Her room was barely recognizable: it was as if a hurricane had rampaged through the space and the amount of damage seemed unnecessary to kill a single witch. There were various scratches and marks in the walls and overturned furniture, along with several dried splashes of blood and the obvious puddle from where the Overseers and Crispin had found her sitting.

"This is definitely related to my case." I muttered, forcing myself to enter her room and examined the damage more closely. Kisten remained in the doorway behind me, keeping his distance as I squatted next to the dried puddle of blood.

"What gives it away?"

"The spread of the damage. The blood. It looks just like all the other scenes." I motioned to the destroyed room as I stood. "If anyone else had been in here, they would've been killed. Honestly, from this amount of damage to the room, it's miraculous that Justina survived at all. This attack was violent, and it must've taken all her strength to avoid getting killed."

My voice faded as I considered what I had said, my eyes looking to the overturned bed where it now sat against the far wall. There was no way an average Supernatural could have done this kind of damage: we were definitely looking for a strong species, one that a penchant for killing violently and quickly.

"Are... are you done or...." Kisten's voice trailed off as he looked away from the scene, it obviously being too much for him to continue looking at. He had treated her wounds and seeing the environment she had gained them in was probably hard on him. I looked around the room one more time, taking a couple of photos with my phone and scanning the room to capture the scene.

"Yeah. I'll send the scene to Chris for analysis later." I sighed, walking back to him in the entryway and resisting the desire to press myself into him. Yoreile quietly closed the door behind me and I nodded to the witch. He merely looked away, not saying a word to me.

"Let's go. *Der Welpe*[4] is probably suffering." Kisten began walking back towards the surface and I followed him, collapsing into the passenger seat as he started up the car. Kisten placed his hand my leg this time, carefully backing out and on the road. As we sped away from the Landing, I couldn't help but fall asleep to the steady vibration of the engine.

---

[4] German "The pup"

9

I was running through tall grass, the sounds of screams and vicious growling echoing behind me. My sister's body hung limply against me, unresponsive as I dragged her away from the chaos and carnage behind us. I could hear our fellow tribesmen being slaughtered, but I closed my eyes to their plight. All that mattered, all that I cared about was getting away with my sister. If I still had her, everything would be okay.

"Don't worry," I breathed, my panic growing as her blood continued to drip down her body, drenching my simple coverings. I fought my own fear and continued to drag her, refusing to stop. Stopping meant death and I couldn't, wouldn't let her die. Tears started to stream down my face as I moved through the grass, doing my best to keep moving. "I'll be brave this time, no more running. I won't fail you this time."

I glanced down and the body was no longer my sister's, but Justina, her dark blue hair matted with fresh blood. I looked back up and found myself in an endless void of darkness, the grasslands disappearing as I paused with Justina's body. The sounds of my tribesmen dying still echoed in the blackness around me and I glanced around confused.

"Why..." I looked back down as Justina spoke, but it was my sister's voice instead of the witch's. She suddenly jerked her head up, the creature's face a grotesque mismatch of the two women, murderous intent in their eyes. It leapt at me, pinning me down as it tried to strangle me, and I thrashed beneath the creature. My wrist started to burn as I tried to push them off, but they only pushed down on me with more force. The eyes of both my sister and Justina glared at me, burning with hate as they pushed their hands more into my throat. "It should've been YOU who died!"

"NO!" I screamed, waking from my dream drenched in sweat, Kisten holding my wrist. The wooden locket also was warm against my chest, and I could feel my sister's presence, although she didn't speak.

"Are you alright?" Kisten never took his eyes off the road as he released me, the burning sensation fading. I breathed in deeply, blowing the air out through my mouth as I tried to calm myself. The lingering dreads of the dream still echoed in the back of my mind, and I absently grabbed my sister's locket.

"I'm fine, just...a bad dream." I whispered, stroking the wood that kept my sister with me. Taking her locket and placing her soul inside was the last act I had done for her, and it was a decision that I could never escape from. Assured that I would be fine, I felt her presence leave me and I dropped my hand, sighing heavily.

"It's okay." Kisten reached back over, this time placing his hand on my legs. I gingerly placed my hand on his and he smiled, never taking his eyes off the road as I weaved my fingers with his. A tingling of pain spread across my skin as I held his hand, but I ignored it, allowing his soft touch to help pull me away from the terrible nightmare.

"We're here." Kisten pulled into a gated community and after giving the name of the resident, drove in. The houses were nice enough but were much too close together for my liking. I liked to have space in-between me and my neighbors and considering his home, I knew Kisten felt the same way. After turning down a side street, Kisten pulled into the driveway of one of the many houses, and a middle-aged man stepped outside to greet us.

"Thank goodness Kisten, he tried doing it on his own again." The father sounded panicked, and Kisten embraced him, patting his back. The man returned the gesture, the panic and fear plain in his body. Kisten remained calm, pulling away to meet the man's gaze as he spoke.

"It'll be alright, where is he?"

"The backyard." Kisten walked around the outside of the house to a side fence, the father and me following behind. The young boy was in a corner of the yard, trapped in between being human and a wolf. His legs almost looked broken as they were trying to change into hind legs and his face had already elongated into a snout. His whimpering broke my heart as his fur started to break through his skin and Kisten slowly walked up to him, talking softly.

"It's okay, you can do this. You don't have to be afraid." He soothed, half-shifting himself to match the boy. He dropped to all fours, crawling next to the frightened teenager. The boy whimpered again, shuffling into the corner more, fur receding back into his body as he tried to turn back to being human.

"I... I'm scared. I don't want to hurt anyone!" He cried and I could see the tears pouring from his canine eyes. I glanced back toward the house and saw a woman and young girl watching from a porch door. The girl was looking at her brother with concern, and even at this distance, I could see the painful look on the mother's face. I looked back to the father and saw tears in his eyes as well.

"Are you..." I asked softly, and the man turned to look at me, at first with confusion but then shaking his head. He looked to the house, locking eyes with his wife for a moment. His expression turned pained as he looked to the rest of his family.

"No, she's the shifter. I'm human." He tried to smile at her, but it failed to reach his eyes. I looked back to the house, my heart breaking for her. It must've been difficult to watch her son struggle like this, knowing it was her fault her son was suffering, and she could do nothing to help him. The man took a deep breath, trying to steady his voice before continuing. "She's tried to help him, but he gets too scared of the animal taking over. She's never able to get through to him, and it takes all her effort to get him to shift back. We figured with his experience, Kisten could succeed where she failed."

I returned my gaze to Kisten, who was still whispering to the boy, sitting on his hind legs beside him. He was rubbing the boy's back with his furry hand, doing his best to soothe him. "The wolf is a part of you, he won't do anything you don't want. You have complete control."

The teen looked to Kisten, seeing that he was half-shifted as well and Kisten smiled at him. The boy's face filled with concern and he leaned into Kisten, sniffing the air between them.

"It... doesn't hurt?"

"No, if you don't fight it, it doesn't hurt." Kisten soothed, licking the boy's face with his sandpaper tongue. "Your wolf wants to share your world. He wants you to let him in. Your mother's wolf wants to see her son."

"Her son?" The boy glanced at the house to his mother, who raised her hand to the glass, tears rolling down her cheeks. Kisten nodded, following his gaze.

"Yes, Travis. You are your mother's human son, but she also has a wolf son." Kisten hummed. "She wants to share both worlds with you, just like your wolf."

"Mom's...mom's wolf is hurting too?" Travis looked back to Kisten and it seemed as if the Alpha's words were getting through to him. "But, Mom's wolf is so kind. My wolf doesn't feel like mom's."

"Because your wolf is you, and you are your wolf. He's not going to feel like your mother's, but he still won't do anything you wouldn't do yourself." Kisten backed away, getting onto all fours again. "You just have to stop fighting. It'll be okay: I'll be right here beside you."

His words were reaching the boy and he started to calm down. Slowly, the teen got on all fours matching Kisten, closing his eyes. Kisten licked his face again, comforting him and encouraging him to finish.

The boy's hind legs finished shifting, fur beginning to sprout through his clothing as the fabric ripped due to his changing form. Kisten's clothing was made of a special material that allowed him to shift without ripping, and he continued whispering and encouraging the young boy, shifting back to being human as the boy's change was complete. The large wolf that replaced him panted, licking Kisten's face while wagging his tail.

"Travis!" The porch door flung open, and the boy's mother ran out of the house, shifting to join her son. The two wolves playfully circled one another, yapping and pawing at each other. The man wiped away his tears and picked up his young daughter as she came over to him, dragging two robes on the ground behind her. The girl looked to where Kisten stood with the wolves, lovingly scratching their ears.

"Is broder okay now?" She asked, looking up to her father as he took the clothing from her. "No more hurt now?"

"Yes, sweet pea." Her father hugged her tightly, his relief obvious in his motions. "He's going to be fine now."

Kisten walked over, flanked by his two charges on either side and the mother licked her daughter's face as the father placed the young girl back down. The girl turned to her brother and he backed away for a moment before lowering his head to the ground. She walked up to her brother and patted his head before wrapping her small arms around his neck, hugging him tightly.

"Wolf Broder!" She exclaimed, and he whined happily, his tail thumping the ground behind him. Kisten stood next to me as the whole family embraced, the mother and son shifting back to human. The father quickly draped the robes over his wife and son and they all turned to face us, bowing their heads to Kisten.

"Thank you so much, Alpha." The woman spoke, her eyes still shiny with tears as she held her robe tightly. "Thank you for helping my son."

"My pleasure, Rachel." Kisten brushed her off, grasping her shoulders before hugging her tightly. "It's my responsibility as an Alpha and a friend to be there for my pack, no matter how young."

He patted young Travis' head, who leaned into the touch before leaning against his mother. Kisten's smile was soft and fatherly as he pulled his hand away. "You're not afraid anymore, right?"

"It was...weird." The boy admitted, glancing away. Rachel was concerned for a moment, but Travis lifted his head as he continued. "But you were right, I was still me. My body was different, but I was me."

"Of course you were." His mother cooed, kissing his forehead as she pulled him against her. "And I'll always be with you, helping you control your wolf."

"Good." Kisten nodded, stepping back to my side. I stood in the yard awkwardly, feeling out of place with the proceedings. I had seen plenty of newbies who had been afraid to shift, but not being a shifter myself, had never been able to help them. Kisten had probably seen much more of it than me and the expert way he calmed Travis showed his patience and skill. Kisten wrapped his arm around me, nodding to the boy's parents.

"Well, we have other errands to run, so we have to excuse ourselves unfortunately." Rachel raised her eyebrows at Kisten's arm around my waist and looked up to my face, sniffing the air in my direction. I cleared my throat, uncomfortable with her scrutiny.

"Is she new to the pack?" She asked, and I couldn't help but cough to hide my embarrassment as I turned away. I hadn't met many of Kisten's pack: in an area as large as The Capital, his pack had hundreds of members and I mostly stayed out of shifter affairs. I always tried to distance myself from becoming too close with anyone who wasn't a part of Command, because if they ever committed a crime, I would probably have to be the one to put them down. Kisten pulled me closer to him, and I looked up to see him smiling broadly.

"Not yet." Before I could refute him, he turned me around and started walking away with me. Once we were back in the front yard out of their sight, he released my waist and turned to look at me, noticing the incredulous look on my face. "What?"

"What do you mean, not yet?"

"Exactly what I said. Not yet." Kisten smiled, his eyes swirling once again. I did my best to look away, but he grabbed my chin, forcing me to meet his gaze. I breathed heavily from the burning sensation on my face, but Kisten didn't release me. Last night seemed to have caused Kisten to throw away most of the restraint he had previously shown, and he only loosened his grip on my chin instead of dropping his hand all together.

"But Kisten, I'm not a shifter, I can't join your pa-"

"As my mate, shifter or not, You're a part of my pack. My Beta." At him mentioning mate, my heart leapt into my throat, and I looked away from him again. Kisten pulled me closer and released my face, pressing my head into his chest. I could hear his heartbeat and couldn't help the shudder that ran through me.

"Kisten, I can't be your mate. You're still bound by the Oath." I spoke into the fabric of his shirt, hugging him tightly. My own chest ached with my words: I didn't want to turn him down, but I knew that there was more than what we wanted. It was the reason I had stepped back when Kisten decided to pull away: there were other factors that stood in the way of us having a true relationship. I heard his heartbeat quicken at my mention of the Oath and I hurried my next sentence. "My job requires that I don't get too close and I still have the Hunters to worry about. It's too dangerous to be with me."

"You'll have to figure it out: you have the time while I court you." Kisten stated and I looked up to him, my chin still resting against him. He was looking down at me, his expression showing how serious he was. "As far as the Hunters, having you as my Beta puts me in no more danger than being Lucius' Alpha. And the Oath... I'll deal with that when the time comes."

"But Kis-"

"I have tried to restrain myself for far too long and abide by rules that don't serve me or my desires. I have only cared for two people in my long life, and last night reminded me how lonely I've allowed myself to become. I refuse," Kisten paused, leaning down to kiss me deeply, once again setting my mouth ablaze. He gripped me tightly, his longing and desperation evident in his touch and kiss. I was left panting when he released me, my body growing weak in his arms. His voice was soft as he spoke again, lovingly stroking my face. "I refuse to lose you."

With this, Kisten released me and continued walking to his car, leaving me in a daze behind him. Court me, make me his Beta: he had basically done the human equivalent of asking me to marry him. I wanted nothing more than to say yes to him, but there were so many obstacles to that sort of future that he seemed to be overlooking.

'No, not overlooking.' I thought to myself as I followed him into the car. 'Just determined to overcome.'

As we pulled out of the neighborhood and began to head to the hospital, I couldn't help but smile at the thought of Kisten belonging to me.

10

Kisten left me in the waiting room as he walked into the normal Supernatural wing, wanting to find a nurse to help him check Justina's vitals as he slipped on his coat. I stood outside her door, closing my eyes as I prepared myself to see my friend. My mind kept flashing to my nightmare and my sister's body but I shook my head to clear it of those images. Breathing deep, I opened the door and stepped inside.

LeAlexende sat on the opposite side of her bed, dead in the chair. The light on his phone was blinking, indicating unseen notifications. It was a little after two, so I knew he would overpower Death's hold on him soon and I stepped up to Justina's bed, closing the door softly. She was still unconscious, but her breath was steady, as if she were merely sleeping. I noticed the many bandages on her arms and midsection, as well as both of her legs in casts. I noticed her left arm was also in a cast, and I gently touched her right hand. She didn't move in response, and I squeezed her finger, fighting to hold back my tears.

"Wake up soon, Justina." I whispered, moving some strands of blue hair as I kissed her forehead. "Help me punish the one who did this to you, Сестра[5]."

The door opened behind me and I moved to the opposite side of the bed near LeAlexende, allowing Kisten and the nurse to enter. They simply went to work, checking her vitals and running simple checks. The nurse assisting Kisten was another witch, as I recognized him as one Justina sometimes got drinks with. He seemed in pain at having to see her like this, but he acted with full professionalism as he aided Kisten, and never once said a word out of turn. Soon, the nurse left with the blood samples to take to the lab, and Kisten remained, looking over to me.

---

[5] Russian "Sister"

"She's good." He smiled, and my shoulders drop as I released the breath I didn't realize I was holding. "I still want to check the blood work, but she's healing herself well. Tomorrow, we'll probably be able to remove the stitches and possibly her arm cast."

"Good." I nodded, looking to LeAlexende as his energy invaded the room. Kisten looked to him as well as the Overseer awoke, flooding the room with power as he escaped Death's grasp. It always felt so dramatic when an elder vampire awoke: the room flooding with energy, a wave of power as they pulled themselves back from the grave. He looked first to me and then to Kisten, finally picking up his phone.

"Have you been here long?" We both shook our heads as he checked his missed messages, barely acknowledging our answer. "Good, good, I woke up on time."

"Come here." Kisten motioned me back to his side and I walked around the bed to meet him. He placed down his tablet before gently taking my bandaged hand and began to remove the gauze he had wrapped it with the day before. My hand was already mostly healed from the wound he had given me and he nodded, pleased with the results. He leaned to retrieve a small pair of scissors and cut the stitches, kissing my hand before releasing me.

"I'll be back after I get the results." Kisten excused himself from the room, leaving me alone with LeAlexende. I remained silent as I leaned against the wall, unsure of what to do or say. After sending a reply to one of his messages, LeAlexende turned to face me, smiling his cheery smile.

"He's a good doctor, no?" he inquired, and I merely nodded, unable to resist smiling slightly.

"He is. He really cares for everyone." I breathed, looking towards the door. My thoughts turned to Eve and I shook my head, my smile fading. The Overseer gave me a strange look as I frowned, his blond hair shifting slightly. "Almost everyone."

"Ah, you are referring to Luc's new Retainer?" I gave LeAlexende a strange look, as I had never heard anyone dare call Lucius Luc, not even Eve. I guess being an old friend and an Overseer gave him the right, or at least made him feel comfortable enough to do so. The vampire's smile faded slightly as I nodded and he turned his purple eyes to the floor. "I must admit, I am not very fond of her either."

"Really no one is." I shrugged, looking away to a corner. "She doesn't do much to try to change that though."

"Well, she really does seem preoccupied with her own ambitions." I was surprised how well LeAlexende had been able to read Eve despite only having met her a short time ago. "But Lucius has always had varied tastes and she's not his first ala Retainer. She just seems...a bit more ambitious than the ones Lucius has chosen in the past."

"How long have you known Lucius?" I queried, my curiosity getting the better of me. The caramel vampire ignored me at first, still engrossed with his phone screen. LeAlexende's smile widened as he looked back up to me, and he was genuinely amused.

"Since he was turned. Like him, I'm one of the First and a former member of her court." I looked at him shocked and stepped back a little. My reaction only seemed to amuse him more, although I saw a hint of pain at my discomfort. "Unlike Luc, I changed...my identity after I left Mater Vitae. I have no desire to be reminded of my past."

"I-"

"I also know you have changed your name multiple times over the centuries, leaving your previous past behind." He interrupted me, not giving me the chance to speak. His eyes bore into mine despite his warm smile and I could almost feel his pain. "I'm sure you understand not wanting the burden of a previous life."

I nodded solemnly, grabbing my sister's locket again through my shirt. Those who did not have immortality or long lives failed to understand the burden a name could carry. Just that single word could wound you worse than any weapon and bury you in the sins and grief of the past. Names carried power and choosing a new name or leaving one behind was always risky. My sister rose at my touch and LeAlexende's gaze drifted to my hand.

"Ah, so you still wear it." I looked at him surprised, dropping my hand. LeAlexende laughed slightly, checking his phone again.

"Lucius is polite enough to pretend he doesn't remember when you were at her court and I doubt he's told your secret to anyone but me. To be fair, it's not as if we really knew you anyway, with the distance she kept you from everyone."

"No one was given the chance." I commented, and my sister drifted away again without saying anything. I knew she was probably still watching me, waiting until I was alone to voice her thoughts. "To Mother, I was a precious pet, only to be appreciated for the rarity I was. I am incredibly grateful to Lucius for his protection and the risk he is taking with me."

"Yes, he is taking a great risk, agreeing to have you in his clan, but he took it a step further and added you to Command." LeAlexende agreed and he checked his phone as it vibrated. "But he always was one to do so. Adds thrill to such a long life."

"What about you?" I asked, and the Overseer laughed slightly, answering his message before looking back up to me.

"Oh no, not me. Just like with changing my name, I prefer to live free of regrets or burdens." LeAlexende smiled his relaxing smile and once again, I couldn't help but return it. "I enjoy my simple life as an Overseer, providing protection and safety for my charges as best I can."

"Is that why you pretended not to recognize me?" I pushed, and the vampire nodded, looking to the ceiling before closing his eyes. I realized how little I knew about so many of the First: all I truly knew about them was their names. I had seen some of them at times, but I could barely put a name to the few I knew by appearance. It was no wonder that I had approached Lucius without realizing who he was and how meeting LeAlexende had not stirred any memories. My voice was soft as I spoke again. "Thank you for helping me, LeAlexende."

"Please, call me Alex or Alexende. Speaking of helping," he opened his eyes, glancing at his phone before returning his full attention to me. "I can tell you confidently that there were no empousa present at any of your crimes, before or after. All the locations are far from any Overseers protecting one and none were traveling through those areas at the time of the murders."

and the shifter hugged me tighter. "I'd hate to see you scar such a beauty."

"Don't worry, I'll take good care of her."

"See that you do." LeAlexende smiled at both of us brightly and settled into his chair. With this, Kisten released me and still holding my hand, led me out of the room. He didn't say a word as we walked through the waiting room, but I recognized something in his gait was off.

I opened my mouth to ask him as we stepped on the elevator, but Kisten swung me into the wall, quickly pressing the button for the lobby before pressing his body into me. The burning sensation on my wrists as he pinned me to the wall told me clearly where his intentions were and I struggled to free myself. Kisten put a stop to this by kissing me, burning my lips and tongue once more. There was no sandpaper texture to his tongue, so once again, his animal was not behind this assault.

"Did LeAlexende guess," he released me from the kiss, interrogating me as he nibbled on my neck. I tried to strain away from him, but he held me firmly in place, the pain radiating from my wrists to my hands and arms. He growled against my skin, the sound beginning to excite me. He noticed the change, as he shoved his knee between my legs, kissing me deeply again. I closed my eyes as I melted under his torture. "Or did you tell him?"

"He guessed." I moaned, the intense pain overwhelming my senses. Kisten released me just as we reached the lobby and I collapsed to the floor as the elevator stopped. He stood me up as the doors opened and he led me through the lobby. I knew he wasn't done with me when we reached his car and instead of releasing me, he opened the door to the back and tossed me onto the seat. Kisten climbed on top of me and closed the door, pinning me again.

"I highly doubt he guessed that much." He growled again, and I saw that his fangs had yet to appear. There was no sign of Kisten's animal and knowing this was all him was just as exciting as it was terrifying. I had never seen Kisten angry, but he was balancing his anger with his desire, as he kissed me deeply again, undoing the front of my pants. I moaned loudly into his kiss as he slid his hand to touch me, the heat almost too much. The underwear Kisten had found for me was much thinner than the pair I had been wearing, and I could feel the more intense heat that the previous pair had protected me from.

"I told him some of it, but he did guess." I admitted as he pulled up from me and he grinned, licking my face and dragging his tongue down to my neck. The searing fire that followed his tongue caused me to moan again and he pressed his hand into me more, forcing me to try to squirm away from him and his painful touch. However, Kisten already had me pinned to the door and I had nowhere to go as he pushed my underwear to the side, and easily slid his fingers inside me.

I cried out at the first wave of pain as it washed over me, and Kisten silenced me with a kiss, drinking in my pain as he moved his fingers inside me. The pain was overwhelming, and I felt as if I would pass out, but I also couldn't deny the pleasure of having him touch me. Feeling him flex and move his fingers deep inside me made me whimper at the intense pain and pleasure, and I couldn't help as I squirmed beneath him.

After what seemed like eternity, he finally released me, sliding his fingers from me and pulling back from his kiss. I gasped for precious air as the pain stopped and I ached from the echoes of the heat. Kisten raised his hand to his face, playing with my juices on his fingers before placing them in his mouth, closing his eyes as he indulged in my taste. I felt a clench inside my midsection and despite the pain it had caused, I couldn't help but want his fingers back inside me.

"You are really enjoying this." He laughed darkly, gazing deep into my eyes as he removed his fingers from his mouth and I merely panted in response, still unable to speak. His gaze softened for a moment and he carefully leaned over me, sniffing my skin. "How hurt are you?"

"I'll live." I breathed, getting my breath under control. "I'd love a warm bath to get rid of this ache though."

"I'll draw you one as soon as we get home." Kisten smiled at me and I smiled back, reaching to touch his face.

"It is interesting to see a different side of you. A passionate side." I admitted and he chuckled, leaning away from me. He almost seemed worried as he gazed at the foggy window.

"You're seeing a repressed side." He sighed, running his clean hand through his hair. "Something about yesterday...unhinged me. I feel like I'm losing all my careful control that I've built up over the centuries."

"It's good to just let go every once in a while." I smiled, settling into a more comfortable position on the seat. Kisten leaned over me, sliding his hand up my shirt as he kissed my neck, once again setting my body on fire with pain. I was beginning to grow used to the heat and it was starting to be less painful and more pleasurable each time I was subjected to it.

'*He really is making me a masochist.*' I thought to myself as I strained my neck to give him better access. He used his free hand to slide my hand down to his erection and I squeezed him through the fabric of his jeans. He moaned into my skin, and my body grew more excited with his sounds.

"Even if all I want to do is bury myself inside you, consequences be damned?" He moaned, his voice strained as he spoke. I carefully undid his jeans and slid my hand inside, stroking him through the fabric as I had earlier. His underwear was already wet from his pre-cum and I gulped, holding in my own desire as I stroked him, teasing him with my fingertips.

Kisten's breath above me grew heavy as I stroked him and he pushed himself up, meeting my gaze. It was somehow more arousing, looking into his eyes as I stroked and teased him. He almost looked as if he was in pain and his soft moaning gasp made me want him even more. I slid my hand into the silk fabric, setting my hand on fire as I grasped him. Kisten let out a loud gasp and he thrusted into my hand involuntarily.

Despite his passion and desire, the fact that Kisten was a virgin was obvious without his animal to guide his behavior. The look on his face, the soft moans at every movement of my hand, the awkward, uncertain thrusts were all signs of someone who was not used to being touched by someone else. The more he squirmed for me, the more I wanted from him: I wanted to make him mine and mine alone. I knew my own eyes had begun to swirl with power as I stroked him more, wanting to push him over the edge, to have him release his seed into my hand.

"Raiven." I could feel his climax building and every part of me craved his release. Kisten had dropped back on top of me, his breathing labored as he drew closer and closer. He gripped my shoulders tightly and pressed soft kisses into my neck with each moan of pleasure. The pain in my hand and arm was intense but I refused to slow down, my selfish desires pushing me to ignore it.

Kisten suddenly bit my shoulder and I moaned with him as he came, his warm seed spreading all over my hand and arm. He thrusted into my loosening grip, spurting more of the warm fluid on both of us. Finally finished, he completely collapsed on top of me and I slid my hand from between us, exhausted from the pain as I let it hang off the seat.

"Gods, Raiven..." His voice was soft when he spoke and I couldn't help but chuckle at his awed tone.

"Realized what you were missing?" Kisten chuckled as well, the deep sound vibrating through both of us. He slowly pushed himself up and lifted my clean hand to his groin. To my surprise, he was still hard, with no sign of softening. My surprise must've shown on my face as Kisten laughed again, releasing my hand.

"Just makes me want you more." He moved from on top of me, shifting my legs until they lay across his lap as he sat on the seat. He took in a deep breath and let it out shakily, clearly trying to calm himself down. He patted my legs as he closed his eyes, still trying to steady his breathing. "Let me get us home so we can actually clean up and I can get you that bath."

"Sounds great." I closed my eyes as he redid his jeans and climbed out of the car. I settled in the back seat as he reentered on the driver's side and started it up, driving us back home.

11

I lounged in the warm water, gently blowing on the bubbles that surrounded me. As soon as we had gotten home, Kisten had drawn my bath, taking a moment to use his shower while the tub filled up. I had fallen asleep on the drive back to his house and awoke as he finished undressing me. Kisten said nothing, merely picking me up to place me in the warm water and kissing me before leaving again.

Kisten was taking a moment to go by my house while I bathed, breaking Lucius' rule, but I knew he would be fine. The culprit really had only been interested in Justina: otherwise, there would've been plenty of other opportunities to attack any of us. A frown started on my face as my thoughts shifted to the case.

"Sis." I felt her consciousness rise as I called out to her and I settled further down into my bubbles. She sat quietly as she had done all day, still not speaking to me and I blew into the bubbles again. "What's on your mind?"

'*About what?*'

"Anything. Everything. The case." I closed my eyes, sighing as I thought of the man who had been by my side for the greater part of a day. "Kisten."

'*Hmph.*' she grunted, and I could hear a lecture in her voice. I winced involuntarily: lectures from my sister had never been pleasant, even when she was alive. When I had been alone at Mater Vitae's court, all she ever did was lecture me. About how I should've been using my power to escape, how I shouldn't have bound her to a locket, how much she...hated me for being chosen to live. My guilt began to rise again as flashes of my nightmare flicked through my mind, and I knew she felt it, as her voice was soft when she spoke again.

'*Well, the whole Beta thing sounds like your problem. I have no say in that, although we both know what you want.*' She sighed, and I could envision her leaning back in a chair, crossing her legs. I smiled slightly and I could hear the smile in her voice as she continued.

'Kisten is probably my favorite of all your partners. You two are nice compliments to one another.'

"I thought you liked Rurubelle." I giggled, remembering a previous girlfriend of mine. I could almost feel my sister's embarrassment as she grunted. "You said she was good for me and I was a fool to give her up."

'Well, I wouldn't have.' she pouted, and I laughed out loud, lifting some more bubbles in my hand to blow on. *'But, again, I'm stuck in a locket. I can't have anyone.'*

"I'm sorry." I dropped my head again, the nightmare ever-present in my mind. My guilt over my sister's death was one I could never escape from, as a constant reminder hung around my neck. That I had been chosen to live, while she had died. "I want to fix it, but we already-"

'Stop it Raiven. I've told you before, I have already moved past this. Your guilt will eat you alive if you let it.' She sighed, clearly upset over my reaction to her joke. I stayed silent, fighting tears that wanted to flow as she continued. *'You did what you could at the time. I may have hated you for it originally, but I have had more than enough time to get over it.'*

"I couldn't be without you."

'I know, but at some point, you're going to have to let me go. I know you have always been...more dependent than me, but I won't last forever.' She stated, and I knew she was right. Despite still being alive in some capacity, I knew she was fading. She slept more often than ever before, and now neither of us could remember what her name was. Little by little, her soul was slipping away and even if I could find a way to give her a body again, she probably didn't have enough of her soul left to keep it alive. I could give her peace by returning her to where she was buried, but I wasn't ready to give her up.

From what I remembered of my human life, my sister was always the more independent and braver one out of the two of us. We had lost our parents young, although neither of us remembered how or why, and the other tribesmen had accepted us, but never raised us. It always felt that they knew we were different somehow, even if they didn't know or understand why. It was almost a revered fear that made them keep us around, and less that they wanted anything to do with us. My sister raised me, tried to help me be brave, but my fear of dying and danger always made me run. Even when I was trying to save her life, all I could do was run.

'*As far as your case,*' my sister spoke again, dragging me from my memories with her voice. She seemed to understand that I was sinking into the past and was trying to bring me back to the present. '*You're making it too complicated.*'

"Too complicated?"

'*Yes, as usual.*' she groaned, frustrated with me for not seeing it from her perspective. '*You're so sure there's a glorified reason your culprit is killing and trying to tie the victims together in a way they don't belong. The motive is obvious if you look at it from the mind of a simpleton. Justina's attack proves that.*'

"Why else would you..." My voice trailed off as I realized what she was saying. "No unified reason, but individual? Simple, petty..."

'*Not everyone will overlook a slight.*' She reminded me and I jumped out of the tub, wrapping the towel around me as I hurried into the bedroom. I snatched my phone off the bed, quickly plugging in Liel's number and waited impatiently for her to answer. My sister remained for a moment, but then faded back to sleep, humming her delight at my understanding. I finally heard Liel's soft, raspy voice on the other end, and she sounded distracted.

"What is it, Raiven? Do you need Crispin?" She sounded as if she was having difficulty keeping her voice down and I wondered if it was time for her to scream again. Banshees had to scream every once in a while to keep their power under control, just like shifters shifted to keep their animal in check.

"No Liel. I just need to know if you and Justina have gone to The Dream lately." I impatiently tapped my fingers on the sheets as Kisten walked into the room and was confused by me being on the phone. I motioned for him to sit as Liel hummed with thought. Kisten sat on the bed next to me, waiting patiently for me to finish.

"No, I haven't gone with her lately. Haven't really been in the mood." I heard a male voice in the background and assumed it was Crispin. He almost sounded out of breath, as if he had come back from exercising. "Actually, Cris says him and her go every Thursday. That's rude, invite me some time."

Crispin must've said something else rude because I heard Liel slap him. He laughed in his usual annoying way and I merely sighed on my end.

"Did they meet anyone, anyone Justina could've upset or made angry?" I waited as Liel repeated my question and my anxiety grew as I heard nothing on the other end. I could hear slight whispering before Liel addressed my question.

"Cris says no, but he wasn't there the whole time. She got upset with him over something and he left early. He said she stayed at least another hour by herself before she left." Without saying more, I thanked Liel and hung up, immediately dialing Lucius. Kisten opened his mouth to speak but I stopped him with a handwave, returning my attention to my phone.

"Hello?"

"Lucius." I spoke quickly, determined to follow the path of logic my sister had put me on. "I need the surveillance of The Dream from Thursday night."

"Done." Lucius said and I think he could tell from my tone that it was related to Justina. I could hear him standing from his seat, and quickly walking down a hallway. "I'll go get the tapes now, Crispin and Liel will bring them."

"Thank you." I hung up again and this time Kisten spoke before I could stop him. He had moved closer to me on the bed and seemed as if he had something important to say.

"Raiven, wait a mome-"

"Not yet." I handwaved him again as I dialed my boss's number and waited impatiently for it to ring. When he answered, I heard the busy sounds of a restaurant in the background and remembered it was Sunday. Brandon must've taken my warning seriously and went to dinner with Arkrian and from the tone of his voice, was enjoying himself.

"What's up Raiven? What can I do you for?" he sounded pleased and I smiled slightly, glad that he had taken the initiative.

His love for his daughter was real and I was happy he had put his prejudices aside, at least for one evening.

"I hate to interrupt you when you sound like you're having a good time but-"

"You were right, this lad isn't half bad." Brandon interrupted me and I sighed heavily, upset that he didn't let me speak. "Did you know that he has a background in football? Even played in college. I thought shifters avoided spo-"

"Yes, I am aware." I exasperated, my annoyance growing. "But I didn't call to talk about Arkrian. I have a new idea on the case."

"What is it?" All the joy in his voice faded, replaced with the seriousness I was used to. I spoke, standing up from the bed and pacing.

"I think we're looking at the case all wrong. The killings aren't connected in the way we were thinking." I stressed, motioning to Kisten, who handed me the new clothes he had bought me from my house. I could see the annoyance on his face from me interrupting him as he handed them to me. I entreated him with my expression as I continued speaking to my boss. "Can you have Julia and Chris gather all the surveillance they can from any night clubs, bars or similar locations any of our victims may have visited?"

"What are you thinking?" He was intrigued by my suggestion and I sighed heavily as I began to dress, carefully placing my phone on the bed. "We've already poured over hundreds of hours of footage and found nothing."

"That he's a revenge killer." Kisten's expression changed as I said this, and I saw something dark flash across his face. "I think he's killing people who have slighted him or offended him in some way. He's going after a specific person and everyone else is collateral damage. He knows he can kill them, so he just does. It's not about numbers or killing certain species or anything. Just that person, and anyone else unfortunate enough to be there."

"Fuck, you're on to something." I heard Brandon as he waved down their server and asked for the check. He was apologizing to Arkrian before giving me his full attention. "That makes complete sense. It explains the randomness of the killings, why they're so spread out. Why some attacks had more deaths than others and why Justina was targeted alone. Dammit that's so simple."

"Yea, he kills the person who slighted him and then," I paused as I pulled the shirt Kisten had bought me over my head. "He leaves to avoid getting caught."

"I'll call Julia and head to the office with her. I'll get Chris to start reaching out to the other Overseers to get us the additional footage." I heard the rush of wind as he stepped out into the night and hailed the valet. "See if you can find out where Justina has been in the past week. She's our best chance of getting a description of who we're looking for."

"Already working on it." I heard the knock on Kisten's front door downstairs, and he looked at me as I motioned for him to go answer it. His eyes narrowed as he walked away, and I couldn't help but be confused by his reaction as I returned my attention to my phone. "I need to go so I can check the tape. I'll be to the office as soon as I can."

"Keep me updated." A click on his end and I slid the phone into my pocket, walking downstairs to find Kisten, Crispin and Liel all in the kitchen. As I came down, Crispin held up the flash drive containing the surveillance and I hurried down the last few steps.

"Lucius said this might be related to your case and what happened to Justina." Liel whispered, keeping her voice low. The banshee was wearing her usual garb: a long, black cloak that hid her form and her white dreads flowing from underneath the hood. Her dark grey eyes were at home on her nearly black skin, and she tugged on her hood nervously. She looked to the flash drive and then back to me, her expression dreary. Crispin handed the drive to Kisten, giving him a nod. Kisten took the drive and walked back up the stairs, speaking quietly.

"Laptop's in the office." I watched him leave and then returned my attention to Crispin, taking in the vampire. With him here, I couldn't help but still wonder what he had wanted to say to me in the garden before we were interrupted. He was looking at Liel, but at noticing me looking, turned to face me. His expression was serious, none of his cockiness or playboy attitude.

"How is she?" He whispered, and I realized that he probably hadn't seen her since Lucius and LeAlexende had carried her away. Liel also looked worried about Justina's state, so it was obvious Lucius hadn't told anyone about her progress. I took in a deep breath, meeting their gaze.

"She's alright, Kisten says she's healing herself subconsciously and he'll be able to remove some of her stitches tomorrow." Both were relieved at my words, and I heard Kisten coming back down the stairs as I continued. "Hopefully, she'll wake up soon but I'm hoping the footage will help us find the one who did this before that."

Kisten set the laptop on the counter and we all hovered around him as he plugged in the drive and opened the file. The footage began at midnight Thursday morning and Kisten began to scroll through the video.

"We arrived around ten." Crispin offered, watching the time stamp in the corner. "I don't know what time it was when I left, but probably after midnight."

"Stop it when they get there." I insisted, and Kisten obliged, stopping the video after Justina and Crispin walked into frame. They sat at the bar together and ordered their drinks, with Crispin immediately turning to flirt with a girl next to him. Liel and I rolled our eyes at the same time, both turning to look at Crispin in unison. The vampire in question merely shrugged, not bothered by our looks.

"Double the speed." I ordered and once again Kisten obeyed, and we watched with anticipation. The night was normal enough: the dance floor was packed, and people came and went from the bar. Justina remained at the bar all night, drinking her drinks as Crispin flitted back and forth. Then Crispin approached Justina, laying a hand on her shoulder, which she angrily shoved off. "There, slow it down."

We all watched in silence as Justina angrily gestured at Crispin, clearly done with his constant back and forth. Crispin appeared to be trying to defend himself, but Justina sat back down, ignoring him as she ordered another drink. He tried to talk to her for a little longer before he gave up and left, heading back for the Coven.

Shortly after her blowout with Crispin, Justina finished her drink and stood to leave as well but was stopped by someone.

It looked to be a woman and Justina was clearly excited to see her, embracing her guest tightly and giving her a kiss. The woman was tall, with skin slightly lighter than mine and she was attractive, showing off her toned legs with her short dress and heels. They sat down at the bar together and I reached around Kisten to pause it.

"Do any of you know her?" All three of my companions shook their heads as I took a screenshot and resumed the video. Shortly after the women sat down, they were approached by another party, a man who was wearing all dark clothing. He had his back to the camera, so we couldn't see his face as he talked to the women. Everything was fine at first, with him even buying the girls more drinks. However, he must've said something Justina didn't like because she seemed to excuse herself from the situation.

The man was trying to stop her, but Justina was making it clear she was no longer interested in being around him. Her friend was also trying to convince Justina to stay, motioning for her to sit back down, but Justina was having none of it. She brushed her way past the man, and he reached to grab her. Crispin hissed as he watched, all of us knowing how bad of an idea that was.

The man was immediately blown back into the bar, finding himself in Justina's previous seat as she turned to glare at him. The man was still facing away from the camera and moved to turn around. I held my breath, my hand hovering to pause the video as we waited to see his face. The bartender stopped him, however, making it evident how bad of an idea it would be to pursue Justina, who was now leaving the bar using the front door. Her friend was trying to get the man's attention, but he stomped off, leaving the same way Justina had. She sighed, finishing her drink and paying before walking out. As she turned, I paused the video again, got the best angle of her face we could, and took another screenshot.

"Send those to me." I demanded, leaning away from the laptop and Kisten obeyed, sending the files to my phone. I accepted the images, nodding to myself. "If we can find that man, we find the one who hurt Justina. That woman and the bartender were the only ones besides Justina who saw his face."

"The bartender's Josh." Crispin added, looking to Liel. She shot him an angry glance and Crispin winced slightly. It was clear she blamed him for leaving Justina by herself but for once, I found myself on Crispin's side. Justina was stubborn and she had decided she was done with him for the night. If he hadn't left on his own accord, she would've made him. "But he went out of town Friday to see his mother."

"Well, his trip will have to be cut short." I spoke bluntly, turning to look back to Kisten's computer. "I'll have him brought into the local division so they can question him."

"Meanwhile, I need to get these stills and this video to my team." I ejected the flash drive from Kisten's laptop and started to walk around the breakfast bar when Crispin caught my arm. I whipped around to glare at him. "Let me go."

"Wait a moment. I–"

"No." I stopped him, pulling my arm from his grip. Kisten also turned to face Crispin, his face dark. Crispin ignored this and shared another glance with Liel, who turned away, not offering him any assistance. I narrowed my eyes at the pair. "What is it?"

"I have to...tell you something. Just you." His demeanor from the garden returned and my suspicion and confusion increased. I crossed my arms across my chest and interrupted Kisten, who started to stand.

"And it has to be now? I want to find who did this to Justina." I argued and Crispin looked away again, this time looking to the floor. "The longer I hold off on this, the greater chance this guy moves again and we lose him."

"I know, and I want to catch him too." Crispin curled his fists and then released it, visibly trying to calm himself down. "I want to do more than catch him. But I have to tell you before she wakes up."

I eyed Crispin, trying to guess his motives. It didn't seem like this was something he wanted to do: unlike the previous day, where he had played his games before attempting to tell me, he now seemed as if he was being forced. I glanced to Liel, who only met my gaze for a moment before looking away again. She clearly was in on what this was all about, and why Crispin had to tell me before Justina woke up but was keeping her distance as usual. I returned my gaze to Crispin who shuffled uncomfortably.

"And it has to be now?"

"Yes." He replied curtly. I placed the flash drive back on the counter and motioned for Crispin to follow me. Kisten and Liel watched our moves, both of their expressions unreadable as I walked out into Kisten's backyard. It was starting to get late in the afternoon and the sun was already low behind the trees. As soon as I closed the door, I rounded on the vampire.

"Now tell me what the hell this is about because if it's just to tell me you're sleeping with her or something, I swear to the Gods I'll end you." I hissed and Crispin looked away from me, not meeting my gaze anymore. He was smiling wryly and honestly looked like he'd rather be anywhere but in this backyard with me. We remained this way for a moment, and my frustration was only growing.

"She made me swear an Oath to tell you before she saw me again." He whispered and I had to lean in to hear him. His voice held echoes of different emotions, but mostly anger. "That's why I wasn't with her when I should've been, or none of this would've happened. I should have just told you in the garden, but I-"

"Tell me what?"

"That she's pregnant." He breathed, and I froze to the ground I was standing on. I waited for him to say he was joking and laugh his cocky laugh, but he remained silent. When Crispin finally looked up to me, his expression was unreadable. "And yes, I'm...I'm the father."

"So, all that in the garden was...." I let my sentence trail, clearly not seeing the connection. He ran his hand through his golden hair, closing his eyes for a moment. "Was to tell me that?"

"She knew you hadn't forgiven yourself over me turning and she didn't know how to tell you herself, lest it felt like she was betraying you. It was her idea for me to tell you in the garden. She wanted you to see that Mikael was still a part of me, even if I don't remember that life." Crispin frowned and then chuckled. "She never told me anything about us before you did, even though I suspected there was more to her wanting to keep her relationship with me a secret. All she would say is that it felt wrong for her to be happy with me the way I was. Well, mostly happy."

I stood awestruck, taking in what Crispin was saying. It was like Justina to think that way, especially since I didn't know she had any sort of relationship with Crispin, much less romantic. I told her all my regret and guilt concerning Crispin and it would only make sense that she would feel guilty for actually preferring him the way he was now. I dropped my head into my hand, still trying to make sense of it.

"So, explain to me why you acted the way you did in the garden." I insisted, gesturing with my free hand. Crispin stiffened, clearing his throat. "I know children are a big deal to vampires, but that doesn't explain why you didn't just tell me without the games."

"That was, uh...mostly just me being me." He flinched as I lifted my head, my eyes glowing with power. "Mostly, Raiven. Justina wanted you to see that I wasn't just an asshole, but I...I guess some part of me wanted that too.

"I know you don't like me, and I'm not asking you too. Lucius wants us to be civil and I accept that's why he didn't want you to tell me. I'm not Mikael: I'm not the guy you fell for." He sounded sincere, and his voice sounded like he was pleading with me. I released my power as he continued. "I like my freedom, to flirt around as much as I want, to have whomever I want. But I also really do care for Justina and she gets me, accepts me in a way most people don't. I do have a concept of commitment, just not yours."

I remained silent at this, unsure of what to say. Crispin took this as a hopeful sign, as he stepped closer to me and gently touched my arm. I didn't pull back, and so he pulled me into a full hug, holding me close. After a moment, I returned his hug, and his body relaxed. He breathed deep into my hair before speaking again.

"You don't have to feel guilty anymore, Raiven. You didn't ruin me." He whispered and it wasn't until I realized his shirt was growing wet that I recognized that I was crying. I thought I had gotten over losing Mikael, that I had forgiven myself for not being there the night he was turned, but when I was forced to face who he had become, I realized how much I was still holding on to the past. I vented to Justina and Liel frequently about my frustration, my disappointment, and my guilt over Crispin, and despite that, Justina never said a word to him about his past. She waited for me to do it, waited until I was ready to try to move past it and then wanted me to see that I was wrong.

"I'm sorry, Crispin." I spoke in his chest, not ready to release him. "I...don't think I'll ever like who you've become."

"You don't have to."

"But," I continued, pulling back slightly to look up at him. "I think I can accept it now and move past it."

Crispin smiled down at me and leaned down as if to kiss me. I let him, and he placed a soft kiss on my forehead, lips barely brushing my skin. When he pulled back up, he had a soft smile on his face and his eyes were shining with tears of relief.

"I'm guessing she can't be far along." I breathed after another moment, releasing him completely and wiping the tears from my eyes. Crispin stepped back from me as well, his soft smile evolving into a full grin, full of happiness. This only lasted a moment before his smile faded and he looked away, gripping his arm tightly.

"She's not, but if you could..." His voice trailed off and I nodded, understanding what he wanted me to ask. Kisten had not considered a pregnancy test at the time, considering her state, but it wouldn't be too much for us to check the baby for him. Besides, there would be other concerns, including Nosferatu Syndrome and Kisten could easily address these early on now that we knew.

"Let's go back inside. I still want to drop the evidence off at the office and Kisten can take you guys to the hospital now that he needs to check Justina again." Crispin raised his eyebrow at my suggestion.

"You know you're supposed to stay together?"

"It's fine." I waved him off, turning to walk inside. After a moment, I heard him follow me. "We know this is a revenge thing, and he's not targeting us in Command or anything. It'll be fine."

Kisten and Liel were still in the kitchen, watching us as we returned. Liel looked to Crispin, who merely nodded at her. The dark-skinned banshee sighed, smiling as she leaned into the counter, her eyes drifting to me.

"Should've told her yesterday." She jabbed and Crispin winced, but he was smiling as he moved to hug her.

"And forgo all the dramatic tension?" He laughed as she tried to evade his arms and I couldn't help but smile as I stood next to where Kisten sat. While Crispin try to plant a kiss on Liel, who was actively pushing him away, I laid my hand on Kisten's shoulder and ignored the pain as he touched my hand. I looked down to find him watching me, his eyes calm. I started to remember that he had wanted to say something earlier and opened my mouth to ask when I was interrupted by Crispin whistling.

"Looks like Justina and I weren't the only ones hiding our relationship." He finally released Liel, who scratched him as he let her go. He hissed at her, but she merely shrugged, turning away from him. I immediately released Kisten and cleared my throat as I looked away. Crispin then turned his attention to the Alpha, leaning across the counter to be eye level with him. "Finally found a Beta? I thought you enjoyed being by yourself."

"Not all of us like to lick every cupcake first." Kisten replied smartly and Liel had to cover her mouth to hide a giggle. Crispin laughed openly, standing back up with his usual gravitas.

"What can I say? I'm a man who likes his dessert." At this Kisten stood, and it looked for a moment as if he had something to say, but the two men merely locked hands. Crispin seemed legitimately happy for Kisten as he shook his hand. "Glad you found someone who can deal with you."

Kisten chuckled, releasing his hand and heading back to the stairs, pausing to kiss me as he walked past. I touched my burning lips as he walked up to the bedroom to retrieve his keys. Crispin laughed out loud at this, throwing his head back as he howled. Both Liel and I looked at the vampire in question, who was wiping away tears.

"God, who knew that man could be jealous?" He squeaked out through tears, wiping away the pink fluid. Upon noticing my confused expression, he did his best to quell his laughter. "I came to Lucius shortly after he became an Overseer. Kisten had been here the whole time and never once have I seen that man be with anyone, much less jealous. I thought maybe he wasn't into people, or whatever you guys call it nowadays."

"Asexual." Liel and I spoke at the same time and Crispin nodded, getting his laughter under control. He moved to turn on the kitchen light as it grew darker outside, bathing us all in light once again. Liel giggled slightly in her corner, meeting my gaze as I looked at her.

"I'll admit it, I thought that too." She shrugged, gesturing toward Crispin. "I think most people have that opinion of Kisten. He almost never talks to anyone: in the past fifty years I've been here, you're only like the second person I've ever seen Kisten hang out with."

"Who was the first?" I jumped at the question and both Crispin and Liel gave me a confused look, as if I should've known. Liel opened her mouth to answer when Kisten's arms wrapped around my middle, startling me. He cleared his throat, interrupting the banshee.

"We should get going." Kisten kissed the back of my neck before letting go, walking toward the front door. Liel looked as if she was going to still answer my question before deciding against it, following him out. As Crispin and I trailed behind them, I couldn't help but wonder what the banshee had been going to tell me.

12

"Hey Raiven." I looked up from my desk as Julia leaned over me, watching me scroll through the video on my computer. As soon as Kisten dropped me off, I passed off the screenshots and video of Justina's night at The Dream to Chris and began working on other surveillance videos that he had managed to get access to. Many of the Overseers were more than willing to work with us, providing everything we needed as quickly as they could: they wanted this solved just as much as we did. I paused the video I was working on and looked over my shoulder to her.

"What's up?"

"We got in contact with Josh, that bartender from The Dream." She smiled, and I turned around in my chair, waiting for her to continue. She leaned against the wall opposite of me, a bright smile on her face. "The local division is questioning him now and Justin and Brandon are joining remotely. Hopefully, he can confirm your theory and get us that visual."

"The footage already does that." I turned back to my computer, zooming in on the frame that I had paused. It was clearly the same man that Justina had met in The Dream and Julia gasped as she recognized the form of the man. "This is the third time I've found this man talking to a victim. He is most certainly our killer, but I can't see his face clearly in any of these videos."

"He must be doing that on purpose. He probably looks for the cameras to avoid them." Julia concluded and I nodded, letting out a frustrated sigh. Technology had advanced so much since I had started doing this and still we couldn't identify a killer from a video. Julia shook her head, clearly sharing my sentiment. "We would need video of the first victim, before he would have thought to hide his face."

"Yea, but we don't have a connection for that first crime." I sighed, leaning back in my chair again. "That was the one that took place in a coffee shop in broad daylight. Eight people died, including the cashiers. The only survivor was the manager, who was in his office with the door closed. Guess he didn't think to check there. Or didn't care."

"Yea, and as far as we've been able to discover, not one of those victims had visited a bar, club or similar environment leading up to the massacre. Even the café's surveillance doesn't show this guy showing up before the killing, so he must've met his target somewhere else." Julia continued and I nodded. She frowned, clearly trying to piece the puzzle together in her mind. "But if they met on the street or something, we'd have no way to tell who the target was. And now that I think about it, why don't we have a video of the killings?"

"The camera was destroyed during the attack, remember?" I reminded her and she closed her eyes in thought. The local division had been so upset about it, that they almost didn't want to tell us. We still hadn't been able to determine if the camera being destroyed was premeditated or simply a consequence of the violent attack.

"So, we really have nothing about the first one, not even the gender of his target."

"Nope, because he seems to go after men too." I stood, turning to face her, walking away from my desk to find Chris. Julia followed behind me as I continued my train of thought. "We also need to determine why his switch was suddenly flipped. Why he suddenly decided to start killing. The way this guy gets turned down, insulted or humiliated, there's no way the café was the first time that ever happened."

"Because he got away with the first one?" Julia offered and I shrugged, not slowing my stride.

"Possibly. We weren't called on until the third killing and now, with Justina's attack, we're up to six. The time between killings has been on a steady decline, so he's definitely been getting more confident. We're really on a tight schedule to find him before he leaves again." I knocked lightly before opening the door. Chris was still running the woman's face through our database and smiled at us as we walked in.

"Still searching." He glanced at his computer, watching the images fly by. "I've checked if she was human as well as all of our suspected races with no match, so we can rule out her being the killer."

"Not yet." I interrupted him, remembering what LeAlexende had told me at the hospital. "It's possible our killer could be a hybrid and we can't rule out that this woman and the guy may be a pair."

"But she hasn't shown up in any other locations, has she? Just the male from what I've noticed."

"Can't rule out that she's a shapeshifter species." I insisted and Chris nodded, seeing my line of thinking. "It is safe to assume that this would be her actual appearance, as Justina recognized her when she arrived. She was too friendly with the man at The Dream for that to be the first time they met."

"Alright, I'll shift my focus to shapeshifting species." Chris paused his current search and started to change the perimeters in the search bar. I nodded as he started the new search, more pictures flashing next to our sample image. He turned to Julia and me, shooing us out of his office. "There's no need to stand around, I'll call a meeting as soon as I get a match."

Julia and I had to hide our laughter as we left, closing the door behind us. Chris was by far the most excited when it came to Supernaturals and was our team's current specialist. He was also a textbook nerd and was not comfortable around people, often staying holed up in his office and not coming out unless a meeting was called. If he had known how old I was, I'm sure he would've loved to sit me down and bleed me dry of my knowledge. However, only the Director knew the truth, and as far as my team was concerned, I was human like the rest of them.

"Hey," Julia stopped walking, her expression lost in thought behind me. "Just a thought, but wouldn't he stay until he could kill Justina?"

"What do you mean?" I asked, and she gestured in the empty air between us.

"I mean, wouldn't he be upset about not getting to finish her off?" she reasoned, and I crossed my arms, completely turning to face her. "I mean, he's always successfully killed his target since he started. That's why he's kept doing it: he's had a taste of retribution and he loved it."

"Except Justina, who somehow survived." I added and she nodded, still lost in her own thoughts.

"Right. I don't think he'll leave town until he gets her. It's almost a matter of pride at this point. He managed to kill more than fifteen people last time, but this time couldn't even kill a single witch?" Julia had a point and I hummed as I thought of a response.

"That is possible, but-"

"Um, Raiven?" Julia and I were interrupted as the receptionist called out to me, and she was a bit frazzled as she stepped back into the office. I gave her a concerned look and she tried to pull herself together, her voice still shaking. "Um, the Alpha is here to see you. He says it's important."

I groaned out loud, rolling my eyes. I had told Kisten to call me before he came back to pick me up but it was obvious that my preferences weren't on the table. Julia continued back to her desk as I walked up front with the receptionist, seeing Kisten in the lobby by himself. He must've left Liel and Crispin at the hospital, which made sense. Both had been impatient to see Justina for themselves and I would imagine now that they had delivered the video, the pair was no longer interested in being with me or Kisten.

"Raiven." Kisten didn't give me a moment to say a word, immediately grabbing me. His tone was both worried and hurried and his eyes were swirling with power. "We need to get back to the Coven now."

"Shh, Kisten, not so loud." I dropped my voice and giving the receptionist a smile, moved Kisten to the opposite side of the lobby. He looked over to her and back to me, confused by my reaction. I leaned him down, speaking to him in a hushed tone. "No one here knows that I'm more than human, that's part of my agreement."

"The woman is at the Coven. The one from the video." Kisten whispered and I raised my eyebrows in surprise. "She was asking Lucius for protection. Says she knows who did this to Justina."

"Then I need to get Brandon and bring her in-"

"Lucius has her locked up in the Basement." Kisten hurried and I understood his impatience and concern. The Basement was only meant to hold those Lucius had deemed a danger to others and having her down there meant he would not give her up so easily. I sighed, frustrated by this news.

"Why?"

"He doesn't want to risk that she's the one who did this. He says he'll only give her up to you guys once you have the man in custody as well." Kisten glanced toward the receptionist before looking at me again. "She's a lamia, originally from the west coast."

"How do you know she's there?" From the way he was speaking, it clearly wasn't Lucius who told him, and Eve never would've offered that up for free, especially if it would help me. Kisten groaned, clearly not seeing how this mattered.

"Aurel called me." His tone was annoyed and worried and he gestured toward the door. "We need to go, before Lucius does something to her and you lose the only lead you have."

"Okay, okay." I sighed, and Kisten fidgeted, clearly in a hurry to leave. I gave him a curt nod as I walked back toward the office. "Give me a second to update Brandon and I'll come with you. I'll only be a moment."

"Hurry." I walked back through the security door as Kisten sat down, clearly antsy in the chair. I made directly for the interrogation room, where Brandon and Justin were still questioning Josh. The poor boy was terrified on hologram and was fidgeting as he spoke. I couldn't blame him for his fear: it was likely that Lucius could blame him for what happened to Justina, even though he had no part other than being present. However, he was a shifter and therefore a part of Kisten's pack: there was no way Kisten would allow any harm to come to him, regardless of Lucius' anger.

I knocked on the door, getting Brandon's attention. He glanced back at the glass and despite not being able to see me, I knocked against it. He excused himself from the projection and quietly slid out the door to see who it was. He clearly was not expecting it to be me, as his tone was surprised as he spoke.

"What, Raiven? I'm in the middle of-"

"Lucius has the woman." I spoke, making it evident that there was no time to waste. Brandon cursed under his breath and he completely stepped out into the hallway as I continued. "She's a lamia who's not from this area, so he refuses to release her until we have the guy in custody."

"But we don't know if she's involved beyond Justina." He reasoned and I nodded.

"I know, but Lucius is not going to risk it. Lamias are shapeshifters related to empousas, so it would be hard to be sure. Besides, I don't think Lucius cares if she's involved beyond Justina: She's involved *with* Justina." I countered and he cursed again, clearly frustrated. "I just came to let you know the state of things. I'm heading there now to see if I can convince him to at least let me talk to her."

"Go. The kid's agreed to give us access to his memories and we're waiting on the tech. Hopefully, we can get the visual of him soon." I immediately turned and left, almost jogging through the office as I made it back to Kisten. Julia called my name as I ran past, but I ignored her as I stepped back into the lobby. Without a word Kisten stood and opened the door for me, and I glanced around for his car, not seeing it in the parking lot.

"Where..." I didn't get to finish speaking as Kisten padded up next to me, fully shifted into his leopard form. He rubbed his head against my hand and laid down, clearly waiting for me to get on. Kisten must've been truly worried about what Lucius would do, as it was dangerous for him to roam the city in animal form. He was one of the few shifters who could do so without being spotted, but it was still only something he did when he was in a hurry. I hopped on the giant cat, grabbing onto his fur tightly and pressing myself against him. He stood and took off into the night, heading for the Landing.

As the wind rushed past us in the cool night air, I couldn't help but hope we could reach Lucius before the worst happened.

13

I leapt off Kisten's back as we arrived at the Coven and he shifted back to human as I started down the stairs. I wasn't surprised when Aurel and Grace met us in the hallway, hurrying along behind us as we rushed past them.

"Him and Eve are currently out, they just left Nirvana." Aurel sounded out of breath as we reached the second set of stairs, Kisten and me not pausing as we continued down. Nirvana was one of Lucius' clubs on the other side of town and it would take him a good while to get back to the Coven. "I don't know how long it'll be before they get here. Lucius is absolutely fur-"

"I'm not waiting, he can punish me later." I asserted, letting Kisten pass me so he could open the door to the Basement. Only one of the Three or someone with their permission could open the door, so I was truly lucky to have Kisten on my side. "There was no telling what Lucius will do to her once he comes back, and I'm not willing to risk losing my only lead to catching the one who hurt Justina."

"Alpha..." Grace's voice trailed off as she fidgeted behind Aurel and Kisten turned to face her as he finished opening the door. His expression softened and he nodded curtly. Grace sighed with relief, clutching her shirt as she quickly ascended the stairs. I was confused by their interaction but turned to enter the dungeon.

When we arrived in the Basement, it was as if I had stepped into a different era. The walls were lit with torches and before me was a hallway lined with stone cells, iron bars holding in the inhabitants. I had never been in the Basement and even now, I wanted nothing more than to run back up to the safety of the surface as Grace had done. The medieval atmosphere of the dungeon only brought back horrible memories of my first few years away from Mother and fleeing her Hunters.

Steeling myself, I quietly walked past the cells, only glancing for the woman. I knew most of these people deserved to be down here: to be in the Basement was considered a fate worse than death.

Anyone down here had hurt someone else in the area or betrayed Lucius' trust: they would be down here until the day they died, or until the day Lucius finally decided to kill them.

"There." Aurel pointed to a cell in front of me and I could hear a woman's cry as we got closer. "That's where she is."

"Kisten, go back up. See if you can talk some sense into Lucius once he arrives." Kisten obeyed, nodding as he went back, disappearing into darkness as he ascended the stairs. I stopped in front of the cell Aurel instructed, the vampire hovering close behind me. It was indeed the woman from the video, but her lower half was no longer human. She leaned against the wall, tears evident on her face as she sat coiled on her beautiful brown tail. Her scales flexed as she looked to me, a sad expression on her face.

"Are you here to punish me?" she asked softly, barely lifting her head from the stone. She leaned against it again after I shook my head. "You should be. I don't deserve kindness."

"What's your name?" I dropped my voice, doing my best to sound professional and polite. She dragged herself from the wall, slithering across the floor to meet me at the bars. She raised herself to my height and we looked deeply into one another's eyes. She must've trusted what she saw there, because she dropped herself back down, sitting on her coils again before she spoke.

"Irida."

"Why are you in Decver?"

"I'm here with my boyfri-" she stopped herself, sighing as she began to cry softly. I grabbed the bars that separated us, pulling myself closer to the barrier.

"Is he the one who hurt Justina?" she visibly flinched as I said this, and her next response was low and full of her tears.

"Yes...no...yes." she looked up at me again, tears flowing down her face. Her top was soaked, indicating that she had been crying for a while, probably since Aurel had brought her down here. "I...you have to help me."

"Why do you need help?" I asked softly, dropping to my knees to meet her gaze. She looked away, as if she couldn't bear to look at me. She started to openly sob again, the sounds echoing through the stone hallways. I pushed my hand through the bars and she took it, squeezing it tightly. "Has he threatened to hurt you? To kill you too?"

"No, yes." she stammered. "Not outright, just...I swear, I didn't know what he was doing at the time, it wasn't until Justina that I realized-"

She stopped as the door to the Basement flew open and from the electricity in the air, I knew Lucius had arrived. I released her hand as I stood, and she slithered back into her corner, terrified of the Overseer. I readied myself as Lucius came into view, both Eve and Kisten trailing behind him. His blue eyes were practically glowing, and his calm face did little to hide his obvious anger.

"Raiven." He stated my name and I fought the urge to kneel, ignoring his silent command. Eve looked at me shocked, her gaze turning to Lucius as I disobeyed him. The Overseer continued up to me, standing over me as I remained on my feet, refusing to back down from his gaze. Kisten and Eve stopped a distance away from us, standing side by side. "You cannot take her."

"I am not trying to." I fought my legs as they tried to buckle, and I stomped my foot, planting my legs apart. Lucius' expression did not change but the electricity in the air changed as he shifted the charge. "I am questioning her."

"There is nothing to question." He stated, and the lamia whimpered in her cell, understanding that he would not help her. I glared back at Lucius as I summoned my own power, my green eyes starting to swirl as the stone around us began to drip with moisture. Lucius raised his eyebrow at this. "Are you challenging me, Raiven?"

"I am." I growled, the air growing damp and heavy as I summoned my power to challenge his. It was starting to get difficult to breathe between the electricity and humidity, but I would not back down to Lucius. My own behavior was slightly surprising to me, but I pushed these thoughts away as I spoke. "I will not allow you to hurt her."

"*You will obey me.*" Lucius' face changed, visibly showing the anger he had kept hidden behind his facade. All of our hair stood on end as the charge in the air increased. I raised more of my own power, the humidity reducing the effects. Lucius scowled at me and even Eve backed away from him, almost cowering behind Kisten as she started to lose grip on her human form. Her horns started to peak out from her hair as she whimpered but Kisten ignored her, keeping his eyes on me. I could tell from his expression that he was clearly worried but I was unwavering in my conviction.

"I will not." I insisted, refusing to look away from Lucius' eyes and the glow in his eyes grew brighter with his anger. "And you cannot make me. I *will* question her and I *will* get the information I need."

Lucius seemed ready to raise his hand against me and I readied myself to retaliate. I heard Aurel behind me step back, clearly wanting to get away from the struggle between me and Lucius. Eve shared his sentiments, grabbing Kisten for protection as her tail appeared behind her.

"Rai-"

"Lucius." Kisten interrupted him and Lucius paused, his eyes still locked on mine. Kisten took this as a good sign and took a step closer, forcing Eve to release him. His movements were slow and cautious as he reached out to his friend and Overseer. "This is not how we agreed to do things. Raiven is just trying to do her job."

"Justina-"

"Will be fine." Kisten insisted, still moving closer to his friend. The glow in Lucius' eyes wavered for a moment, but his gaze didn't move from mine. I backed down a bit, recalling my power as Kisten continued. "Blood for Blood, but not this. If you kill or harm this woman, she'll never catch the one who actually attacked Justina. This is not how we wanted to do things: we agreed to never do things Mother's way."

Lucius closed his eyes at the mention of Mater Vitae and he seemed as if he was taking Kisten's words to heart. His eyes still glowed when he opened them again, but the charge in the air had lessened. I still met his eyes, waiting to see what he would do. He glanced to Irida, who cowered under his gaze and she shifted into the corner more, as if trying to escape him. His eyes softened for a moment, and I ventured a chance to speak.

"By all means, keep her. She wanted your protection anyway."
I suggested, and Lucius returned his attention to me as his eyes
narrowed. I fought the urge to cower and took a deep breath. "I just
want to question her and get whatever I can from her."

"Then question her." Lucius relented, standing against the
wall across from her cell and motioning Eve and Kisten to his side.
Kisten immediately moved to his friend's side and Eve reluctantly
obeyed, leaning against him as he wrapped his arm around her.
Taking a deep breath, I turned to face Irida again, dropping to my
knees.

"Irida." She jumped as if struck when I called her name, and I
spoke more softly. "Please, Irida, I need you to tell me what you can."

"I... I can't." she whined, hiding in her corner more as she
started to sob again. "He has a spell on me, I can't act against him. I
can't even say his name anymore."

"He's a witch?" I coaxed and she nodded, turning her teary
eyes to me. She seemed to have some determination despite her fear,
and she was trying to figure out what she could say.

"I swear I didn't know. I thought he was a normal human."
She moaned, trying her best to speak between sobs as she chose her
words carefully. "I didn't know he was using me to do...to do...those
things..."

"Wait," Kisten interrupted me, and she jumped at the sound
of his voice, turning away again. "He rolled you?"

"Yes." She wailed, being sent into another crying fit. The air
charged around us again and I turned to Lucius. His grip on Eve had
tightened and he was looking at Irida darkly as she cried. I was
stunned into silence as she wailed, her tears having long since dried
from the lack of water. I glanced at Kisten and I knew we were
having the same thoughts: a witch that could mind control a human
was one thing, but one who could do the same to other
Supernaturals was dangerous beyond reason.

"I didn't know what he was doing, I didn't know he was using
me for my ability." Irida suddenly flung herself into the wall, the
sound of her body colliding causing a crack that made my stomach
turn. Kisten didn't hesitate as he threw open the bars and rushed in

to check on her. Her arm was bleeding, and Kisten reached for the sheet that laid on the simple bed, tearing it to make a bandage. Irida was covering her mouth as she tried to calm herself down, and she looked to me, begging me with her expression. It was clear that it was the spell that had caused her to hurt herself and she was frantic to find the right words. "He said we were going on a road trip and I didn't think anything of it. Ju...Here...I...I realized when I saw Justina..."

"You stopped yourself." I stated and she nodded, covering her mouth again. Her beautiful brown eyes were red from her tears and she pulled in a shaky breath. She was truly trying her best to help me, despite the obvious danger to herself. I curled my fingers in anger as Kisten checked her arm to make sure nothing was broken. I had to close my eyes and take a deep breath before I could speak again. "That's why Justina survived, why no major organs were damaged. You were able to overpower him once you realized."

"To overcome means to be aware. I was never aware of what was happening. I think he always waited until I was asleep. I only realized he had taken precautions when I tried to tell Justina." She lamented, slithering away from Kisten and back up to me, taking my hands again. "She.... tried to help me. That's how she got hurt. She was trying to keep.....it...from killing me while he was trying to regain control of..... Eventually, when they came to the door, he gave up and Justina told me to hide."

"Where have you been all this time?" I spoke soothingly, stroking the back of her hands. Irida hiccupped as she tried to control her emotions, chancing a glance at Lucius. He was merely watching her blankly and she returned her gaze to me. I hushed her, trying to help keep her calm. "It's okay, just tell me."

"I've...been here the whole time." She admitted, her body shaking from fear. "I didn't know how to leave. I don't even know where here is, so I stayed hidden in Justina's room. I came out when I knew he was trying to roll me again. I knew there were people at the door and I needed someone to help me.

"Please, I don't want to hurt anyone, I don't want to kill anyone!" she screamed, grabbing my hands and squeezing them up would be mandatory. This guy is too dangerous and too cunning if he can roll other Supernaturals, so only someone of Command would be strong enough to resist him."

Lucius nodded and looked to Aurel, who stepped back to join us. He merely knelt to Lucius and started towards the stairs that would take him above ground. Lucius released Eve and started after Aurel but was stopped by Kisten.

"A moment?" he asked and Lucius agreed, motioning for Eve to go up without him. She hesitated as if she wanted to argue, but decided against it, merely glaring as Kisten walked further into the Basement with Lucius, out of earshot of us. She turned her attention to me and glared.

"I bet you just love this, getting to be the one to solve this case." She hissed and I ignored her, starting toward the stairs. I had enough of the dungeon and while I felt bad leaving Irida alone, I couldn't stand the idea of staying. Eve stomped after me, her anger radiating off of her. "It should've been the local team: it should've been me."

"There's no glory here, Eve." I huffed, climbing the dark stairs. She scoffed behind me, turning me around once we reached the Coven. Her horns had started to appear again and I met her gaze evenly. "All that matters is stopping this lunatic so he can't hurt anyone again. Doesn't matter who does it."

Eve merely hissed at me and I pulled myself from her grip, climbing all the way up to the surface, checking my phone for a signal. She paused as if she was going to follow me, but decided against it, turning down another hallway as I closed the door. I leaned against the wall as I waited for signal, my thoughts turning to poor Irida.

'I'll get him, for both of you.' I swore, calling the office as soon as my service returned. 'He's going to regret this dearly.'

14

After putting the finishing touches on my plan with Brandon and the team, I hung up, closing my eyes as I leaned against the building. I glanced at my phone as it reminded me of its low battery, sighing heavily. I peeled myself from the wall and walked to my car, which had been sitting since I left with Kisten to the hospital.

I started her up and plugged in my phone, closing my eyes again as I waited for Julia to arrive. I had told her what Aurel looked like and to meet him in front of The Dream, but I wasn't sure if he'd be there. She was supposed to call me if she couldn't find him and I sighed again, lifting my phone to check the time.

The bright screen told me 9:45, and I knew The Dream had opened a short while ago. I doubted our suspect would come tonight, but we couldn't rule out the possibility of it happening. Thanks to her refusal of him, he had to know that she had betrayed him, and depending on how impatient he was, it was possible that he would do whatever it took to find her.

I looked up as the door to the Coven opened and I saw Kisten step out. I had been curious as to what he wanted to talk to Lucius about, but it was obvious that it was private, and not something he wanted to share. My thoughts drifted to his annoyed behavior while Crispin and Liel were at his house, and I readied myself to face him as he looked around for me.

"Here." I turned off my car and opened my door, motioning him toward me. Kisten walked toward me and I was slightly worried as he pulled me out of my car and closed the door. He wrapped his arm around my waist, and I glanced around worriedly. "What are you doing? What if someone sees-"

I was interrupted as he leaned down to kiss me, and for the first time, no intense heat and pain followed. Surprised, but not wanting to let the moment pass, I wrapped my arms around him as he pulled me closer. I let my tongue dance across his lips, enticing him to let me in. He did, and I almost moaned at the sensation of our tongues sliding against one another without the usual pain distracting me. He almost seemed to be trying to drink me in and I let him, clinging to him as we kissed.

"Kisten," I gasped, pulling back after what seemed like eternity. "Why didn't the Oath affect me?"

"Till sunrise." He smiled, hugging me close as if I'd disappear if he let me go. His voice caressed my skin as he spoke softly against it. "Until sunrise, you and I can be lovers."

'So that's what you asked Lucius.' I smiled, hugging him tightly, silently thanking Lucius for this small gift. "How did you talk him into it? How did you talk Eve into it?"

"Being honest. I told him I wanted to make you my mate and court you correctly." Kisten shrugged as he pulled me towards the back door of The Dream, and I pulled against him slightly. "Asked for one night free of the Oath and he agreed. I'd imagine Eve is not happy about it."

"But why are we..." I started, but Kisten pulled me inside and I found myself drowned in bodies and loud music. He pulled me towards the bar and sat me in his lap.

"You are in dire need of a distraction. Let Aurel and your team handle the case for one night." He waved to the bartender, another member of his pack. She bounced toward him and smiled, clearly recognizing her Alpha. "Vodka for the lady and gin for me."

"Of course." She winked at him, a gleam in her eye as she looked at me. As she turned to make our drinks, I tried to slide out of his lap but he wrapped his arms around me to keep me still. Kisten then pulled me higher so that I could know how happy he was to have me there. Just feeling how hard he was, that hardness pressing into my thigh, made me catch my breath.

"I like you in my lap." His voice caressed my ear as the bartender set our glasses down. Her expression told me that she understood her Alpha's intentions and she smiled at me brightly.

"I can tell, but you're letting everyone else know too." I sipped on my glass as he laughed, refusing to look at him as the song drifted into another similar sounding tune.

"They'll all know soon enough." He reasoned, kissing my skin and I sighed with relief. I almost missed the pain but couldn't deny the simple pleasure of feeling his lips on my skin without it. It was as if he was trying to drive me crazy, giving me a taste of what it would be like if I was his mate. If I would say yes to him like he knew I wanted.

Trying to clear my head of these thoughts, I turned my gaze to the sea of movement. If I hadn't known we were in a club, I could've almost sworn this was some type of sex ceremony. I had never been inside a club like this: even when Lucius required me to help, I mostly stayed outside, helping with security. The intense energy and movement was new to me and I wondered what the appeal of the environment was.

Out the corner of my eye I saw a young man walking in the front door and I couldn't help but tense up as he glanced around the club. He spotted me and made a beeline for my seat and as he grew closer, I recognized that he looked nothing like our suspect. Once he saw the Alpha holding me in his lap, he tried to mask his actions and sat two seats away, his eyes still on me.

I couldn't help but laugh and gave him a wink as I took another sip of my drink. I leaned back against Kisten so he could hear me over the noise. "No competition, hmm?"

"I would certainly hope not." He glanced behind us, looking for my pursuer. Upon noticing the man staring at me, he smiled, his fangs visible as his eyes swirled with power. The man quickly left his seat and I glared at Kisten, hitting him playfully.

"You did that on purpose. Poor guy probably wet his pants."

"If he didn't, then he has a big set of balls on him." He laughed darkly, and I gave him a surprised look. I had never heard such vulgar language from Kisten before and it sounded so foreign in his voice. Having finished his own, he took my drink and nearly drained it. He waved for the bartender to refill them, sliding some bills underneath the glasses. "I saw the way you winked at him."

"Whatever." I turned to my re-filled drink, taking long draughts while trying not to ask the burning question in my mind. Curiosity finally won and I dropped my drink into my lap. "Kisten."

"Yes?"

"Were...Are you jealous?"

"Of?" He turned me in his lap so he could see my face, but I gazed into my drink as I avoided looking at him. I couldn't help but remember the dark look he had given Crispin and I suspected Liel had filled him in on the truth about my past with the vampire. His behavior afterwards also appeared to show his jealousy, but I wasn't sure.

"Nevermin-"

"Not really." He answered, raising my face to his. He searched my eyes with his before pulling me into another blissful kiss. He was smiling softly when he pulled back, eyes still locked with mine. "Crispin isn't Mikael. You don't like it, but it seems you've accepted that the person you loved is dead. There's nothing to be jealous of."

"Oh." I mumbled, finishing down my drink. Of course, Kisten would think that way: with Crispin's relationship with Justina, it was clear that we weren't involved in any way. My mind went back to the other person Liel and Crispin said they had seen Kisten be around and I wondered if that had been Kisten's first love.

"Kisten, who-"

"Time to dance." He interrupted me, downing his second drink and spinning around in his seat.

"But," I started to protest, but he was out of the seat and pulling me to the dance floor. He swung me so I was in front of him and wrapped his arm around my waist while his other hand gripped mine. His front was pressed along the length of my back, hips intimately touching.

"Tonight's about me and you." He leaned forward as he whispered in my ear, his voice full of darker things. "No Eve, No Crispin, no case: just Us."

Since I had never danced before, he started out slow and I followed the line of his body. The beat began to move me: soon I was dancing against him on my own. Kisten whipped me around to face him, still gripping my hand as if I'd run away at my first chance.

I wasn't sure why he was so worried: I was strangely enjoying myself at this new way of dancing. It was intimate and enjoyable and reminded me of a time long gone, a time before Mater Vitae.

After a moment longer, I got bored of his way of movement: he was keeping it simple, swaying, and a little rubbing. However, this simple dance was not what I wanted, not what I craved and not what I remembered. I did a slow twist of my hips that grinded my groin against his. His chartreuse eyes lit with fire as I continued my grinding and twisting.

"I thought you didn't know how to dance." I shuddered slightly as he leaned down and his breath caressed my ear. I flicked out my tongue to tease his earlobe and traced it down the side of his face until I found the warm crevice of his mouth.

"I thought I didn't, but this is nothing new to me." I smiled, twisting myself again and he growled, planting a kiss on my forehead. "The music is different, but the movements are the same as my tribes."

"Is that so." Once again, our mouths joined in the darkness of the club as he grasped my hips, moving me so that I grinded against him. With him controlling my movements, the feeling became more intense and I moaned into his kiss. His tongue rolled in and out of mine, mimicking what he wanted to do with my body.

I barely noticed as he moved us across the dance floor towards the far wall and I connected with it softly. Kisten gently stroked my face before kissing me again, pressing himself into me. His body was crushing me against the wall, but I loved every second of this pain-free contact. I moved to wrap my arms around his neck, but he stopped me, pinning my hands to the wall above me as I moaned into his kiss. He pulled back after a moment, his eyes now swirling with his lust and desire.

"Decide now, Raiven." he panted, still trying to exercise some of his careful control. "Because I can't take much more of this before I decide for you."

I couldn't begin to articulate my need for him. I had wanted Kisten from the moment I had met him, and my desire and love had only grown over the past three years I had been in Decver. I knew this was all to tempt me into being his Beta, but we both already knew what my answer would be.

"Kisten," I began, but I froze against him, tension ringing off my body. Kisten lightly shook me but my mind was completely blank with surprise. "Oh, no no no."

"What?" Kisten saw the many emotions flash across my face as my eyes rested on the person at the bar. He leaned across it, his eyes searching as my coworker sat next to him, facing the bartender. Julia's hair was beautifully done and her dress was revealing enough to make me blush, but it was the vampire next to her that had my attention.

"Aurel." I could see Kisten's confusion as I began to look for a way to escape, to get away from where he could see me. I felt as if Aurel would be able to pick me out of the squirming crowd, despite how unrealistic that was.

"What's wrong, he's supposed to be here, remember?" Kisten's confusion was obvious in his voice and I squirmed to free my hands from his grip. He held me tightly however, still refusing to let me go.

"He can't see me like this." I begged and Kisten's eyes darkened with jealousy again as he looked down at me. His growl was barely contained when he spoke again, pressing me into the wall more.

"And why is that? Something I should know about you two?"

"No, I don't-" I stumbled over the words as I tried to explain myself. I looked away to the floor but Kisten pinned me closer against the wall, making it evident that he would not let me leave. I moaned as he assaulted my neck, playfully biting and licking me. "Please Kisten, I just don't want him to see us, this isn't how I want to tell him."

Kisten paused for a moment as he considered my words. Without releasing me, we made our way through the moving bodies along the wall and I knew he meant to take the door leading to the Coven. It was almost as if the crowd was pushing us where we wanted to go: we floated along the wall, effortlessly moving toward Kisten's goal. Reaching the door, Kisten silently opened it and we slipped into the dark stairwell.

As soon as we were in the Coven, Kisten slammed me into the door, assaulting me once again with his mouth as he pinned me against it. The sound of me hitting the door was drowned out by the loud music on the other side and I knew that no one inside was any the wiser to my plight. I moaned openly, my hand grasping his hair as he kissed and bit my neck, working his way down to my collarbone.

"Want to tell me what that was?" He growled, never ceasing his assault on me. I struggled to speak in between my own gasps and moans.

"Aurel, wants me for his harem." I managed and Kisten paused, standing up straight to meet my gaze. His eyes swirled with a mix of desire and anger and this time, I knew his jealousy was real, unlike the mix of emotions he had shown towards Crispin.

"And?" He spat the word out, no longer touching me sensually but keeping me against the door. I would've preferred his anger from the hospital to this: he loomed over me, his presence and anger filling the stairway as he waited for my answer.

"And I haven't told him no yet." I admitted, looking away from his intense gaze. "I hadn't figured out how to tell him how I feel about you."

"And?" Kisten pressed, leaning down close to my ear again, breathing his words into me as I shuddered. I could still sense the anger in his words, but it had lessened with my admission and his desire was winning him over again. "How do you feel about me?"

"I..." I paused, knowing what he wanted to hear. There was so much more than just how I felt about it, but that was all Kisten cared about. He had to already know what my feelings were: my actions over the past day had more than proved it, despite my verbal denials. I knew he wanted to hear me say it, to finally hear me admit it to him.

I reached up, cradling Kisten's face with my hands. He let me, his eyes still angry as he waited for my answer. I sighed as I enjoyed the feeling of his skin in my hands, and I couldn't help but stroke his cheek with my thumbs.

"I want you." I breathed. His expression softened at my words, and I whispered my next phrase. "I love you."

"Good." I yelped as he scooped me up and started carrying me down the hallway to his room. I had never been to Kisten's room in the Coven before and barely saw the insignia on the door as he opened it and swung us in. He closed the door with his foot and immediately carried me to the bed. He laid me on it gently, leaning over me as he stroked my face. I wrapped my arms around him again and said the first thing that came to mind.

"Kiss me."

15

I allowed myself to get lost in his kiss, purely concentrating on how wonderful it felt to have him holding me, kissing me, after all the time we waited. His arm was firm around my waist, one of my hands tangled in his brown waves while he kissed me, our tongues dancing in passion's embrace.

Pulling me closer, he rubbed his groin against mine, and a delicious warmth exploded through my body before settling back in my lower region. I let out a gasp and clung to him as he did it again.

"How badly do you want me, Raiven?" Seeing that masculine smirk on his face, hearing the thickness in his voice only proved to intensify my desire and I felt as if I might die if I didn't have him in me at that moment. Knowing the effect his words had on me, he held me against his body, and rubbed our groins against each other again. He continued using his body to pin me 2to the bed until I thought I would fall through it.

"How badly do you want me to be inside you?" Kisten whispered against my skin, enjoying his dominance over me. His words danced over me, flowing like water. "Tell me, Raiven, I want to hear you say you want me."

"This much." I pushed to roll him off me and he let me, laying back on his bed. I slid myself on top of him and relieved him of his shirt. I kissed the crook of his neck as his hands fumbled to remove my shirt and bra. Once he had them off, I slid down his body and with no great ceremony, I pulled down both his pants and underwear before engulfing his bulging erection in my mouth. A gasp hissed from him as I took him in, sucking with deep, rough pulls. His hand found its way to my free one, and he thrusted ever so slightly toward me, forcing me to take all of him in.

I came back off him and took my time tasting his manhood, licking every inch and rolling his jewels in my hand. He moaned softly with my tender touches and I felt clenches deep within my own sex with every sound that escaped his lovely lips. After an eternity, I slid my lips over him again, slowly taking his throbbing member into my mouth. A moan like a sigh flowed from him as I took it all in until my lips met where my fingers still caressed him. I rolled him in my mouth, using my tongue to stroke his shaft and my throat to squeeze his head.

He soon pushed me off him and, sitting up, kissed me hungrily, seeking the wet warmth from our kisses. His free hand sought my breast and played with the nipple, rubbing, squeezing, and pulling. My soft moans made him smile as his lips pulled away from mine and settled on my other nipple. My hands caressed his head as he licked me with his sandpaper tongue and his hand played with its twin. The lack of pain gave me the chance to focus on the pleasure and I moaned loudly, not even trying to soften my voice.

"Kisten," I managed to squeeze out his name and he paused, looking up to me. He panted loudly, his fangs visible and his eyes swirling with desire. Light spots were visible on his skin and I knew his animal was helping to drive his actions.

"Yes?"

"Touch me here please." I begged, moving his hand from my breast to my wet slit. He kissed the crook of my neck as he undid the snap at the front of my pants and slid a finger along my wet crease, rubbing against my swollen opening. I moaned for him again, my back arching. The pain had distracted me from how amazing it was to have him touch me and it was driving me insane.

"This is what you could have." Kisten purred as he slowly slid two fingers inside, and flexed them, watching my face as his actions served to increase my want. My whole body began to throb and pulse with my desire to have him inside me, to have him plunge his hardness into the depths that his fingers now searched. "What we could have."

He continued to tease me with his hand while kissing me, using both his fingers and tongue to mimic what he knew I wanted him to do with my body. Soon my whole body was aflame with my desire for him and I tried to arch away from him, to pull away from his teasing hand and kiss. He wrapped his other arm around my middle however, holding me where I was, forcing me to endure what

I deemed as torture. I wanted him inside me, and I knew he could tell. There was no way he couldn't smell how much I wanted him, how much I craved him.

Soon he broke our kiss to steal a glimpse at my face, and I tried my best to glare, but I couldn't hold on to my annoyance. He smiled and nuzzled my breast and I moaned with frustration. Soon enough he moved his hand away from my wet, pulsing slit, and without the added distraction, I managed a halfhearted glare.

"You're being mean."

"I'm being dominant. I am still your Alpha, Raiven." Kisten growled, kissing my cheek as I turned away from him. "Don't worry. I'll give it to you soon enough."

I began to speak when he stood, picking me up and depositing me back on the bed. Swiftly, he removed our remaining clothing, leaving us both nude against the dark blue sheets. After undressing, he climbed on top of me and poised himself above my opening. However, instead of entering me as I wanted, he continued to tease me, only sweeping the outside.

"My, my, you are quite wet down here." I could hear the strain in his voice, knowing that he wanted to be inside of me as much as I did, but couldn't resist the temptation to make me beg him. I began to squirm, and he had to hold me down, pinning my wrists to the bed.

"Goddamn you Kisten!" I couldn't help but yell my frustration at his teasing. He chuckled deep and low in his throat before pausing.

"Is it really that bad?"

"Yes, that goddamn bad."

"Tsk, Tsk, language." He grinned and leaned over me for a kiss. Even as I kissed him back, I couldn't help my snide smile when we separated.

"Well if you would just fuck me already, I wouldn't have the breath to use such language."

"True." He propped himself up and I was so wet he was able to thrust his full length inside me with one stroke. My hands dug into the sheets as my back arched, and I let out a loud moan as he filled me. Completely inside, Kisten took a moment, his entire body shaking as he enjoyed the sensation of finally being inside me. He leaned over me again, kissing my neck before whispering. "You okay?"

"I'm fine." I breathed, smiling up at him, my eyes half open. "How does it feel to finally lose your virginity?"

Kisten laughed low in his throat again, causing me to clench around him. He loosened his grip on my wrists, planting a firm kiss on my lips.

"Amazing." Raising himself on his arms, he began to move inside me. The flames of passion that had danced in my lower regions now danced throughout my whole body and I couldn't remain still. I began to squirm as my hands searched for something, anything to hold on to, and soon Kisten had to hold me down again, pinning my wrists to the sheets once more.

"Jesus, woman," He shook his head and smiled, his eyes still swirling and his spots lightly appearing on his face. "If you had wanted it this bad, you should have just told me,"

Somewhere amidst the thoughts that racked my mind and the heat and pleasure that racked my body, I found my voice. "I believe I did a year ago, and you turned me down."

"Let me make up for that then." With that, he began to pound himself into me, and my hands freed themselves and found his shoulders. The pleasure was almost unbearable, and yet I couldn't get enough of it. I felt as if I was drowning in it: nothing else around us existed to me, except Kisten and the feel of him filling me. I was floating on a cloud of euphoria and pleasure, and he was the balloon that kept carrying me higher. The muscles in my sex began to contract around him as I started to orgasm, and his voice came out deep and strained.

"God, Raiven, you're going to make me come." True to his word, not long after I came, he thrusted into me and poured his warm seed in my middle. Breathing heavily, he lingered inside me a while before pulling out and laying down beside me. I made it a point to try to control my breathing as he did the same, his fangs fading along with his spots.

"I want more." I said at length, my breath under some semblance of control. The once raging inferno was now no more than a spark, but a spark I had no intention of trying to ignore. "There's still time."

He looked over at me, and upon seeing my serious expression laughed before kissing me. Soon, he pulled back from the kiss and glanced down at his member, which was still erect. "Well, all yours."

I slid my hand down to his slick shaft and kissing Kisten tenderly, I began to stroke him slowly. Allowing him to intensify our kiss as he became more aroused and I moved my hand faster over him, teasing him with my fingers. Once I knew he was ready, I broke our kiss and slid down his body, licking his length before sucking only the head. As soon as my lips touched him, he let out a moan as his hands searched for something to squeeze. I came off him long enough to reach for a pillow and toss it to him before I took him in again, going a little deeper, but not much. I looked up to his closed eyes, seeing the expression of pleasure on his face.

Although I knew doing what he wanted would lead to what I wanted, I couldn't help but want to get back at him for all his earlier teasing. Licking his shaft again and sliding slightly up his body, I placed his erect member in my cleavage and squeezed my breasts together.

"Raiven, what are-" His question was caught in his throat as I began to massage his shaft with my breasts and suck on his head. His grip on the pillow tightened and I couldn't help but let out a little giggle at my small victory.

"I'm getting a little payback." I licked the head before sucking on it again, continuously massaging his shaft with my breasts. Soon after, however, I stopped since my libido argued that this teasing would only slow the process. I wanted, needed him and no amount of teasing was worth waiting to have him inside me again.

"There." I moved away from him, climbing back on top of him. He leaned up and kissed me forcefully, throwing the pillow somewhat to its former place. His spots were starting to reappear, and I could tell that Kisten had less control over his animal this time around. His hands on my body carried hints of his claws and his fangs had already returned. The spots gracing his tan skin gave me an idea and I rolled off him, laying on my stomach.

"Where are you going?" he purred, leaning over and kissing my neck. I shivered as I leaned forward on my hands and propped myself up on my knees. He gave me a questioning look and I noticed his pupils had shifted to feline slits. I nodded, answering his unasked question. At first, he looked surprised and a little torn, unsure if he wanted to follow through. "Are...are you sure?"

"Scared?" I teased and Kisten tried to chuckle, but he shifted on the bed, lifting his body up as he moved behind me.

"A little." He admitted, forcing my legs apart as he positioned himself at my wet slit, brushing my opening. From that small movement, I understood why: in the short amount of time after I released him, his body had changed more than I realized. His member was no longer human shaped, and I couldn't help but be more aroused.

"I take full responsibility." I pushed myself back into him and moaned loudly as he slid inside me. The feeling was slightly painful, and I sank onto my elbows as he pushed himself fully inside me. Although I had enjoyed the intimacy of being able to see his face, I found myself thoroughly satisfied with this more animalistic position. It was evident his leopard was pleased as well, because as soon as he had completely plunged into my depth, he pounded himself into me, clearly no longer concerned about hurting me. His claws dug into my waist as he embraced me with wild abandon, his moans mixed with animalistic growls.

Moans I didn't recognize as my own and sounds I had never made before began to rise from me, faster and louder as he moved inside me, his barbs only serving to rebuild the flame of pleasure that had filled me earlier. Kisten's growls grew in intensity as he leaned over me, and he pushed my head into the bed with his clawed hand. I could feel the heat from his breath as he panted above me, and I moaned loudly as he bit my shoulder, his fangs penetrating deep.

For a moment I wondered if I should try not to be so loud, lest someone heard us, but that moment passed, and I decided I didn't care if anyone heard me. The only thing that mattered was the heat and pleasure that resulted from having him inside me and my hands clenched the sheets as I orgasmed for what seemed like eternity. He began to pound himself into me harder and came inside me for a second time, roaring as he released his seed. It was as if he wanted to fill me with his liquid heat and he gripped my waist tightly as he orgasmed.

Calming down, he gently pulled out and laid down beside me as I remained on all fours, still shaking from the residual pulses that my orgasms left in their wakes. Kisten was watching me with a smile, his fangs peeking out of his lips.

"Had enough yet?" Kisten asked between breaths, obviously tired, his form reverting to human. I fully collapsed on the bed beside him, my body shaking from fatigue. Kisten propped himself up, concerned. His hand touched my shoulder, and he looked at the blood with horror. "Raiven?!"

"Fine." I managed to pant, giving him a quick thumbs up as I laid back down. Kisten jumped up from the bed, rushing into his bathroom so he could dress my wound. I hissed slightly as he squeezed the bite, trying to ensure that I would get no infection from his saliva. His movements were slow, as if he were worn out, but he dressed the bite properly, taping the gauze over the mark.

"Next time, say something." He whined, kissing my shoulder as he finished dressing the wound. I laughed slightly, raising my head to look at him.

"And miss out on that? Never." I blew him a kiss as he gave me an exasperated sigh. "Besides, I'll be all healed by morning from something like this."

"Perhaps." He consented, placing the kit on his bedside table before laying a kiss on my back and resting his head against me. I closed my eyes, sighing happily as he stroked my thigh.

"I love you." His voice was soft when he spoke again and I sat up at this, forcing him to raise his head. My eyes met his and I reached for him, forcing him to slide back up the bed until we were face to face again. His eyes were shining, and he smiled at me softly. My heart pounded in my chest as I took in what he said, cradling his face in my hands. I giggled softly, gently kissing his sweet lips.

"I know." I smiled, my chest aching with how much I loved my Alpha. Kisten purred, sliding us more onto the bed and under the sheets. He intertwined his legs with mine, clearly wanting to enjoy holding me for as long as he could. I buried my face into his chest, breathing him in happily as we settled in to sleep together.

16

I awoke alone in the bed and looked around to see Kisten standing in the doorway to his bathroom, his back to me. I watched him silently for a moment, taking in the view. He had evidently been up for a while: the bathroom mirror behind him was still foggy on the edges and his hair showed signs of dampness. He was fully dressed and engaged in the conversation, laughing quietly at something the other party said.

I sat up slowly, stretching loudly as he turned around to look at me. He dropped his phone away from his ear and smiled at me, moving toward the bed. He covered the mouthpiece with his hand, leaning down to bury his face into my neck.

"Feel free to take a shower." He whispered, and the burning pain from the kiss he planted on my forehead reminded me of how much a blessing the previous night had been. I yawned, taking his suggestion as I slid out of the bed. Kisten hummed with contentment as I walked away and I turned around to find him enjoying the view. He had his phone back to his ear and silently blew me a kiss as I stepped into the bathroom, closing the door behind me.

I turned on the shower and waited, looking to the bathroom mirror as I removed the bandage from my shoulder. I could see finger smudges in the glass and my curiosity grew as I looked at them. I breathed against the glass and revealed what was written: "I love you, *Vogel*[6]."

The words brought a wide smile to my face and I sighed happily as I tried to look at my back. The bite Kisten had given me had mostly healed, and I stepped into the shower slowly, waiting to see if the wound would hurt. The lack of pain was encouraging and I fully stepped into the running water.

---

[6] German "Bird"

As I basked under the warm water, letting it wash away my sleep, my thoughts returned to Aurel. I was still worried that he had seen me and Kisten in The Dream the night before, and I sighed heavily at the thought of having him confront me about it. It was all my fault and I accepted that: I should've told him the moment I realized that his feelings toward me had changed. Even if I hadn't wanted to reveal my feelings for Kisten, I should've at least told him about my lack of interest in him.

"Look at the mess you've made for yourself." I muttered under my breath, reaching to wash my body. I cleaned myself up and stepped out of the shower, seizing and wrapping a towel around my still dripping body. I walked back out into the bedroom to find it empty, with no sign of Kisten anywhere.

A new outfit lay on the bed and I knew Kisten had not gone to my room to get my clothing. The red sundress that lay on the bed for me was nothing that I had ever owned, and I gingerly picked it up, unsure if I wanted to wear it.

"Still having doubts?" I heard Kisten's voice as he stepped back into the room, standing against the doorframe as I held the dress. I turned towards him, still holding it in my hands. His expression was hopeful but wary as he slowly stepped into the room, closing the door behind him. "I won't force you if you're not ready."

"What does me wearing it mean?" I asked, and he smiled slightly, stepping closer to me. My heart pounded with his slow steps and I watched his every move until he stood directly in front of me.

"That I've chosen you." He stated, wrapping his arms around the towel as he held me close, pressing his face into my hair. He took a deep breath, releasing it shakily. "It tells others that I've decided to pursue you."

"How long have you had this?" I wondered aloud and Kisten chuckled, releasing me and stepping back to allow me to get dressed. I stood a moment longer, still uncertain if I wanted to go through with wearing it.

"Would you believe me if I said since I told you we couldn't keep seeing each other?" It was my turn to chuckle as I carefully laid the dress down and sat on the bed to slip on my underwear and bra.

Kisten merely watched me from where he stood, a smile glued to his face.

"So, your immediate reaction was to buy me a courting gift after telling me to go away?"

"Before. I bought it before." He admitted, looking down to the floor. I paused in my movements, surprised by his words. "I bought it on impulse, and that's when...when I knew I was falling too hard for you. That I would only end up hurting you more."

"I wish you had been honest, Kisten." I slipped on the dress, surprised by how well it fit me. I wasn't the type to wear dresses, so it was a little surprising that Kisten had been able to figure out my size. I spoke again as I slipped on the provided sandals to match. "Good guess on the size though. I'm impressed."

"I'm glad." Kisten wrapped his arms around me again, as if it pained him to keep his hands off me. I merely smiled up at him as he rocked me in his arms, smiling like a happy child at me wearing his dress. It warmed my heart to see him so happy and I carefully wrapped my arms around him, avoiding contact with his skin.

"So how exactly is this courting thing supposed to work?" I quizzed again, pulling back from the man holding me. Kisten grinned, holding his hand to his lips.

"Can't spoil all the fun. This is my first and only time doing this." He chirped, clearly pleased and excited. He motioned for me to follow him as he left the room. "Let me enjoy this."

"Fine, fine." I consented, following him and closing his door quietly behind us, took a moment to look at his insignia. As expected, it had a leopard carved into the wood, with a large "A" carved underneath. I assumed it stood for Alpha as I traced the shape. I felt something cold and metal drop around my neck and I looked down as Kisten placed a necklace on me, fastening it slightly above my locket. The necklace was a simple, gold "R" and I turned to look at Kisten questioningly.

"Another courting thing?"

"Yes," He grinned, and it was clear he was enjoying this. "I was going to present it when I got home yesterday but lost the chance with all the stuff going on with your case."

"So, this is what you wanted." I lifted it gently before I let it fall back against my skin. "What does this mean?"

"It shows that I've marked you as my future Beta and none of my pack can touch you or pursue you." I looked at him confused as he said this.

"Isn't that what the dress means?"

"In a way." He admitted, walking down the hall. I followed quietly behind him, waiting for him to finish. "The necklace is a specific sign to my pack: as long as you accept my courtship, you have to wear that at all times. The dress, well, that's just for today. Vampires use a red dress to mark pursuit as well, so everyone will know that you're mine."

Kisten whipped around quickly, wrapping his arms around me again as he pulled me into a deep kiss. I was again reminded by how nice the previous night had been as my lips and tongue ached with pain, but I forced myself to ignore it, doing my best to kiss him back. When he pulled back, his eyes were bright with a fire.

"It also shows that I've finally marked you." He whispered, his voice deep and sultry. I couldn't help but blush as he referenced the night before and he laughed darkly, releasing me. He motioned for me to continue following him and I found myself in the dining room. Sitting on the large table was a breakfast spread for one, and I knew immediately that this was what Kisten had left to prepare while I was showering.

"Is this another courting thing?" I groaned as I sat, Kisten pushing in my chair for me. He shook his head as he sat across from me, smiling brightly again.

"No, just me taking care of you." He chuckled, leaning on his hands to watch me. "I'm allowed to do something nice for you, aren't I?"

I didn't answer, merely blushing and turning my attention to the breakfast before me. Kisten had really gone out of his way, cooking me everything from waffles, to eggs, to bacon and sausage. He even had flowered the fruit, making me almost not want to touch anything.

Eventually, I began to eat and hummed with delight at the delicious food. After a few bites, I looked up to see Kisten still staring at me, his soft smile on his face. I lifted my arm as I coughed to hide my embarrassment, looking away again.

"What is it?"

"Nothing." He shrugged, never taking his eyes off me. I shifted uncomfortably under his gaze and Kisten chuckled softly again. "You are more easily embarrassed than me and I was a virgin until last night."

"It's been a while." I argued, taking another bite of food. Kisten leaned back in his chair, crossing his arms as he waited for me to continue. "I've never been courted before, but I haven't had even this kind of attention for a long time."

"Well, I'll make sure you get plenty of it." Kisten looked away as his phone went off again and he stood, excusing himself as he stepped out to take the call. Finally free of his staring, I focused on the delicious food he had prepared for me. I ate as much as I could and leaned back, quite full of the spread.

'You seem happy.' I heard my sister's voice rise in my mind and I sighed contently, closing my eyes in my chair.

"I am." I said aloud, glancing down at the remains of my breakfast. The flowered orange still sat untouched on its plate and I touched the fruit gingerly. "Kisten has a way of doing that."

'So, you've decided then? You chose to wear his dress.' I frowned at this, sitting up in my seat slightly. I heard my sister's exasperated sigh at my lack of an answer. 'Deny it all you want, but the fact you put in on shows where your intentions lie.'

"I know, I just..." My voice trailed off and I didn't finish my sentence, my thoughts turning to my job, Eve and...Aurel. "It's a little more complicated than just what I want."

'Guess you'll have to figure it out.' My sister echoed Kisten's words as the man in question came back, hanging up his phone call. I was confused by the many phone calls: Kisten wasn't usually one to be on his phone much. He looked at my mostly empty plates and smiled, removing the dishes from in front of me.

"Give me a moment to wash these and I'll get you to work." He promised, disappearing into the kitchen. I smiled, closing my eyes again as I waited for Kisten to finish. I opened my eyes as the door opened, but it was not Kisten I found myself staring at. It was Aurel, who was giving me a strange look in my dress, eyeing me up and down with disbelief. His hazel eyes were full of confusion and they slowly drifted up to meet mine. I stood and stammered to explain myself.

"Aurel. I-"

"Who gave you that dress?" His voice sounded pained as he spoke, as if what he was seeing couldn't be real. The words got caught in my throat and I couldn't say anything as he stepped further into the room, causing me to step back from him. Aurel's expression changed from confusion to anger as he repeated his question. "Do you know what wearing a red dress means?"

"I-"

"She does." Kisten walked up behind me, placing his hands on my shoulders, careful to touch the sleeves. I looked up to see his gaze and he was looking at Aurel, a smug smile on his face. I looked back to Aurel, who was waiting for me to deny it. When I said nothing, Aurel returned his eyes to Kisten, returning his dark glare. "I wouldn't have given it to her without explaining what it means."

"When did this happen?" he sneered and the Alpha behind me chuckled, releasing my shoulders as he walked around the table to stand down the vampire. I was rooted to my spot as Kisten smiled at Aurel, clearly enjoying flaunting this in his face. I wanted to tell Kisten to stop, but the words were caught in my throat. The vampire turned his gaze to me, his eyes dark with jealousy. "Is this why you've been pushing me away?"

"Aurel, I-"

"No. This happened last night." Kisten interrupted me and Aurel kept his gaze on me, waiting for me to deny it. I simply turned away, not able to find the courage to answer that look. Kisten laughed at his reaction, earning himself a hiss from the vampire. "She's wearing the dress, isn't she Aurel? What more proof do you need?"

"You tricked her." Aurel hissed, clearly not wanting to believe what Kisten was saying. I turned to face him at this, shocked by the vampire's words. Kisten shrugged, his grin broadening as the vampire continued. "Raiven wouldn't choose you. She wouldn't lock herself to one person."

"If that's what you want to believe." With this, he turned to me, motioning for me to come to him. "C'mon, Raiven, I need to get you to work."

I carefully walked around the table as Kisten held the door for me, and I kept my gaze from meeting Aurel's as I followed him out of the dining room. Once the door had closed behind us, I took a moment to breathe a sigh of relief. I glanced up to see Kisten looking at me, his dark smile still on his face.

"How was that for him finding out?" He asked innocently and I looked away, still torn about the whole confrontation. I realized that Kisten had probably set Aurel up to see me in the dress, especially after finding out he wanted me for his harem. I started walking away, muttering under my breath.

"Probably as bad as if he had seen us in the club last night." Kisten chuckled at this, wrapping his arm around my waist as he caught up to me. He took a moment to breathe me in before leading me down the hall, heading for the surface.

"Maybe, but I think I like this better." Kisten leaned to plant a kiss in my hair, never pausing in his stride. I was tempted to look over my shoulder, but decided against it, not wanting to see Aurel behind me. Kisten must have noticed, as he did glance back and waved to someone behind us. From his deep chuckle, I could guess who it was as he whispered into my ear. "Hard to think we were once friends."

"Friends?" I repeated, and Kisten nodded, his dark look fading for a moment to a softer expression.

"Aurel... well, he never seemed to be bothered by my distant behavior. Eventually, he reached out to me, saying it looked like I could use a friend." Kisten's expression returned to its dark glare and his smile was full of anger. "Turns out he just wanted me for his harem and was trying to butter me up first. As you can guess, I didn't take it so well."

"Sounds familiar." I muttered, thinking of Aurel's words in the dining room. I didn't want to believe that the vampire had only befriended me to seduce me, but I couldn't deny the possibility, especially with how he handled me choosing someone else. Kisten squeezed my waist, encouraging me to continue. "I mean, Aurel was the one who sought me out to be secret friends, without anyone knowing."

"Sounds like him actually, although he didn't keep our friendship a secret. I'm glad you chose me instead of him." Kisten released me as we climbed up the stairs and I stepped into the afternoon sun. I saw that his car was now in the parking lot and looked at him questioningly. Kisten shrugged, pulling out his keys from his pocket. "I woke up this morning. You're the one who slept most of the day."

"Gee, I wonder why." I remarked sarcastically and he laughed, kissing my hair as he walked past me. I glanced at my car, still sitting in her parking spot. "You know my car is here, I can drive myself."

"Of course you can." Kisten smiled, leaning over his open door as I went to my car to retrieve my phone. I had no missed messages, meaning last night had gone smoothly without our suspect showing up. "But I enjoy having you in mine."

I couldn't help but smile as I closed my door and stepped into the passenger side of his car. As we pulled away, I noticed Aurel standing on the sidewalk outside the Coven. Our eyes locked for a moment and my thoughts turned to what Kisten had said about Aurel's intentions. As we drove away, I couldn't help but worry about the mess I had gotten myself into.

17

I leaned against the glass terrarium, sipping my drink and adjusting my dark sunglasses as the groups of people walked by me. As soon as we had reached the office, Brandon had shooed me right back out: he wanted me to take Julia's place at the Landing, watching for our culprit. She had stayed at The Dream all night with Aurel and was asleep at her house to get ready to do it again. We didn't want to risk him at the Landing without us having eyes there, so I was Brandon's next pick.

We were the only two women on the team and he was hoping we could act as bait for our witch, getting him to approach us on his own accord. This unfortunately would've meant I had to work with Aurel, but a quick call on Kisten's part saved me from my fate. I smoothed my dress, finishing off my beverage and tossing it into the trash next to me.

"Ready to move somewhere else?" Kisten came up behind me quietly and I turned to look at him. He was wearing a dark red button up shirt and khaki pants as well as matching shades to me. A fancy watch finished off his look and he easily blended in with the usual high-class shoppers that frequented the Landing. I was still wearing the red sundress, with the added trappings of a red purse and some gold bangles around my wrists. I was uncomfortable with so much extra baggage but both Kisten and Brandon had insisted it would allow me to blend in better. I glanced at my phone, seeing the time before shrugging.

"I guess, let's shift a little closer to The Dream." I stood up and started walking off in front of him, pretending to be interested in the various store fronts. Kisten walked behind me, glancing for anyone following us. He shifted a little closer to me, leaning down to whisper in my ear.

"Wouldn't you blend in better, if you actually looked like you were shopping?" He offered, and I turned to see the devilish grin on his face. Even with the sunglasses hiding his eyes, I knew his intentions were far from just helping me blend in. I shrugged him off as I kept walking.

"Not really the shopping type."

"C'mon, it'll help you blend in." Kisten stopped my stride and turned me towards a lingerie store. My cheeks burned with embarrassment as I pulled away from him and I could hear him chuckling behind me.

"I guess I could try." I stepped into a clothing store near The Dream and pretended to be interested in various women's clothing. I turned around to see Kisten sitting outside, relaxing on the bench across from the store. I rolled my eyes as I returned to my window shopping, lifting a green halter that was much too short for my tastes.

"Do you need some help, ma'am?" I turned to look as one of the shopkeepers approached me, her fake smile beaming as she waited for my answer. I politely smiled back and shook my head.

"No thank you, just looking."

"Well, let me know if you need anything...else..." Her voice trailed off as she looked me up and down, as if finally noticing my dress. Her eyes worked their way up to the necklace and she glanced outside to Kisten, her eyes widening. Her voice was low and shaking when she spoke again. "You're with the Alpha? A-Are you sure you don't need any help? I can help you find whatever you need. We have the latest in holo-rooms, you can try on whatever you would like-"

"I'm fine sweetie." I tried to smile, starting to wish I hadn't worn the dress. I hadn't expected to run into anyone from the pack and I was still embarrassed by its implied meaning. The girl seemed worried and she glanced back towards Kisten and I followed her gaze. I couldn't tell if he was looking at us or not due to the sunglasses, but just knowing he was there was enough to frazzle the girl, as if we were testing her. I laid my hand on her shoulder and she jumped under my touch.

"Hey, sweetie," I started, and she looked up at me sheepishly. I forced myself to smile brightly as I lifted my sunglasses, looking at her face to face. "No need to get worked up, I'm simply browsing. I'm not really looking to buy anything here. Kisten's not here to judge you or anything."

"Thank goodness." She was relieved as she walked away and I continued my walk through the aisle, not really finding anything that interested me. I eventually found myself in the aisle containing jewelry and I paused for a moment, taking in the latest trends. I was about to walk away when one of the rings caught my eye and I gently lifted it to get a better look.

It was a replica of my opal ring, although clearly costume jewelry and a poor imitation of the real thing. After escaping from Mater Vitae' Hunters, I had lost the ring before recently reclaiming it from a collector. The man had been proud to flaunt it, as virgin rainbow opals were extremely rare and until discovering my ring, most believed that there was only one in the world. Since my ring held the second known stone, the man had been reluctant to part with it before I persuaded him it wasn't worth his life. It didn't surprise me that it would still be in the public consciousness, considering its rarity and recent spotlight.

"*Arcus Pluvius*." I read the tag aloud, a name the public had given it. My memories drifted back to the one who had given it to me, during a time long forgotten. It had been a parting gift, a reminder that he had once existed before Mater Vitae erased him. He had already known that she would not forgive him for his trespass, no matter how special he was. Mother was always creating new species back then and killed off any if they caused her too much trouble. Mother never had an issue using her Hunters to kill off one of her mistakes, but he had been different, and she did the deed herself.

Like me, he had been one of a kind: a Seraph, a being able to manipulate the weather with his flight. Just as she did with me, Mother kept him close to her side and secluded from others in her court.

We were singular successes that she had not been able to replicate and thus we were kept in the equivalents of birdcages: able to be looked upon and appreciated for the rarities we were but never free. I was probably one of the few alive who remembered him, and it had been his death that had given me the nerve to try to escape. Shortly after, the First also rebelled, so it was easy to say that it was his execution that had started everything and led to Mater Vitae retreating to wherever she now was.

"Remembering something?" I dropped the ring in surprise and turned to Kisten who was standing behind me. He slowly bent to pick up the ring from the floor, examining it as he stood. I watched him, wondering if he recognized it. After a while he shrugged, looking at me. "Pretty for a fake."

"I have the real one." I whispered, watching him place it back. Kisten raised his eyebrows as I met his gaze through the sunglasses.

"Wait...isn't that the ring some big shot collector bought at an auction a couple of years ago?" he wondered, and I nodded, beginning to make my way through the store. "I remember Lucius telling me it belonged to a member of Mater Vitae's court before she killed him. No one had known what happened to the ring until it showed up at the auction."

"It was given to me, right before he was killed." I stated, weaving my way back through the clothing. "And the collector was difficult to convince, but I wasn't leaving without it. It had been a gift, a way to remember him."

"You knew the Seraph?" Kisten asked and I nodded, stepping out of the store back into the bright sunlight. I looked up to the blue sky with its soft clouds and smiled wistfully.

"We were similar in our uniqueness and Mother had our rooms close enough together that we sometimes got the chance to talk." I spoke quietly, watching the fluffy clouds as they rolled by. Kisten stood next to me, also looking up. "He was the closest thing I had to a friend in those times. I think he felt the same way, since he gave me the ring."

"What did he do?" Kisten asked quietly and I shifted my gaze to him, slightly surprised. "To be executed?"

"You don't know?"

"I only know what Lucius told me when we left Europe, which is very little." Kisten shrugged, glancing down at me. "I was only about fifty years old when I agreed to come with him, and he has never really been talkative about his time with Mother. The most he told me was it was the Seraph's death and your escape that convinced him and the others that they needed to leave too."

"He revealed the flaw in her system. We both always knew that the Rules didn't affect us the same way, but we had been careful to avoid allowing her to find out." I admitted, looking back up to the sky. "He disobeyed her command, to save someone else from her wrath. Once she realized she couldn't control him, she killed him. I was sure I would be next, so I found the courage to leave."

'More like I kicked your ass but whatever.' My sister rose to make her snide remark, but Kisten interrupted me before I could rebuke her.

"I assume the First rebelled for similar reasons?"

"I'm not sure." I sighed, closing my eyes and turning away from the sky. My thoughts turned to LeAlexende and what he had said at the hospital. "I never really knew any of the First personally, just their names. If I had to guess, I would imagine that they finally had enough of her and after finding out I had managed to escape, figured they could do the same."

"And that's how she lost control?" He asked quietly and I nodded again.

"Yea, the First managed to use her own system against her and began to offer protection to those who didn't want anything to do with her, creating the Overseer system as a more balanced version of hers." I sighed heavily, remembering the turmoil that had followed. The Dark ages had been a time of darkness and madness not just for humans, but for those of us who lived in their shadow as well. "She sent her Hunters after them and me, but as members of the First were killed, other Supernaturals realized they could offer the same protection as Overseers. Hunters still chase after me and any First who remain, but I think she gave up on regaining control when she chose to disappear."

Kisten said nothing to this, following me silently as I weaved through the sea of shoppers and people. I had never dreamed I would have such freedom while I was in Mater Vitae's court and certainly never thought I would've survived as long as I did. Her

Hunters were always searching and never seemed far from my trail. The fact I hadn't encountered any in the past three years was already a blessing, but I had accepted that there would come a day when I lost this millennia old struggle.

'*But not today.*' I thought, turning to Kisten behind me, who paused as I turned to face him. I studied him for a moment before smiling, and he slowly returned my smile. Stepping up to me, he lifted his sunglasses as he leaned down to kiss me and I leaned up to him, despite the searing pain. He smiled softly at me with his chartreuse eyes before dropping the sunglasses back down and walking past me. I couldn't help my stupid grin as I followed, sighing with happiness.

18

I stood amongst the busy people as Kisten stepped into a store, insisting that he would buy me "something appropriate" for blending in with the other shoppers. I started to argue that plenty of people came to the Landing to window shop, but he was having none of it, disappearing into another women's clothing store.

I glanced around the growing crowd, ever watchful to catch our suspect. However, I was soon distracted by the number of couples walking around together, arm in arm, hanging all over the other. My heart ached slightly, but a smile soon grew on my face. I no longer had a reason to be envious of others: it was merely a matter of time before Kisten and I could be the same.

"Raiven?" I instantly froze as I heard the voice behind me and I swallowed hard, refusing to turn around. I could hear his footsteps as he drew closer and I knew that he would not be so easy to get rid of. "Raiven, look at me."

"What, Aurel?" I turned to face the vampire, crossing my arms as I did so. His orange curls bounced, and his eyes still held hints of his anger and disbelief. I was glad for my sunglasses, hiding the uncertainty in my eyes while I did my best to speak with confidence. "Shouldn't you be resting for tonight with Julia?"

"Why?" he begged, and if not for the anger that was hidden in his expression, I might have believed his distress was real. I shook my head, frustrated with myself: I should have noticed this side of him sooner, this possessive side. Aurel placed his hands on my arms, gripping me tightly. "Why him? You...you're not like that."

"Because I love him." I breathed, breaking free on Aurel's grip as I stepped away from him. My actions had caught some attention, but most people kept walking as if they didn't notice. I glanced around before returning my eyes to Aurel. "He's been my choice since I came here, Aurel. Justina was the only other person I wanted, and well...she's taken."

"He's bound by the Oath: You can't have him either." Aurel pointed out and I shrugged, doing my best to pretend this didn't bother me. "He's just binding you into a one-sided relationship."

"Lucius gave him a night free of the Oath to pursue me, I'm not all that worried that he won't free him entirely." My calm tone hid my inner turmoil and for a moment, I was assured in my relationship with Kisten. The confidence was infectious, and I couldn't help my smug smile as I continued. "I didn't have to wear this dress, Aurel. I chose to."

"He is tricking you." Aurel hissed, still trying to convince me to side with him. I laughed, removing my sunglasses from my face as I gave him an incredulous look.

"Tricking me? Kisten has been nothing but honest with me, even when he pushed me away." I glared at Aurel, refusing to look away from his gaze. "I'm not so sure you can say the same. Kisten told me about your pursuit of him, how you pretended to want to be friends to lure him into your harem."

"I have never lied to you Raiven. I did want to be friends with you, and eventually I wanted more than that. I thought you wanted the same." He insisted, stepping closer to me as I stepped back again. My demeanor cracked for a moment with his plea and he immediately moved to take advantage of it. "I admit what I did with Kisten was wrong, but that was long before I met you. Please, Raiven, reconsd-"

"No." I stated plainly, not letting him finish the thought. I wanted to slap myself for being so stupid: I had valued the idea of having a friend so much that I had overlooked the obvious. Aurel was obsessed with his collections, be it jewelry or people and while he treated his collections well, he was relentless when he wanted to add to it. Just as he had begged me for my jewelry, he was refusing to let me slip away from him. "I have made my choice. I made it long before I put on this dress."

"Raiven-"

"Something wrong, *der Liebling*[7]?" Kisten came up behind me, placing his hand on my shoulder as he leaned around to hand me my shopping bag. It felt heavy as I accepted it and I glanced inside to see it full of various outfits. I looked up to Kisten who shrugged as he shifted his attention to Aurel, his dark smile returning. "Ah, come to beg some more? I think she's given you her answer."

"Fuck off, Kisten." Aurel hissed, dropping his desperate act for pure anger. Kisten chuckled low in his throat, gripping my shoulder tightly. I was worried for a moment that he was losing control as his hands began digging into my shoulder, hints of his claws stabbing my skin. I looked up to his face, but his expression was calm, only his burning eyes revealing his emotions.

"Or what? You can't do anything to me, Aurel." Kisten gloated, brushing his hand across my hair before planting a soft kiss. Aurel growled and the semi-interested crowd was now extremely interested, many people stopping to watch the display. I began to feel uncomfortable under their gaze, but Kisten shifted his hand from my shoulder to my waist, keeping me pinned to his side. "I think you should just leave us alone."

"You turned me down, Kisten. I accept that." Aurel said, not trying to appeal to anyone's emotions anymore. He had his eyes locked on me, his pupils boring into me as he spoke. "But you don't have the right to take her from me. She won't be happy trapped in a relationship with one person."

"I believe she told you the truth, Aurel. She chose me long before you decided you needed another 'rare beauty' for your harem." Kisten hissed, no longer trying to hide his anger or jealousy either. It was starting to seem more like a personal vendetta rather than fighting over me and I squirmed in Kisten's arms. "Maybe you should learn to accept not everyone wants you."

"Aurel, please." I spoke again, cutting the vampire off before he could speak. His eyes continued to stare into my soul and I sighed heavily before continuing. "It's my fault, I should've said something before now. Blame me for that if you want, but I never intended to

---

[7] German "My Love"

lead you on or anything. I have never felt more than friendship for you and yes, while I am happy having multiple partners, I'm more than happy being monogamous as well."

"Hearts don't change that easily." Aurel spat, looking up to meet Kisten's gaze. The Alpha smiled, releasing me as he walked up to Aurel, once again using his superior height to stare him down. The crowd was now whispering, and I knew there had to be those present who recognized who we were. All Supernaturals in The Capital had a vague idea of who was a part of Command, and many of those in Decver were definitely capable of recognizing us on sight. I shifted again, holding the shopping bag with both hands as I tried to ignore the burning stares.

"You're right, Aurel. They don't." Kisten's voice was dripping with sarcasm and jealousy as he spoke, his dark smile only widening. "I'll guess you'll just have to wait and see though. Because right now,"

Kisten leaned down into the vampire's face, almost close enough to kiss. He whispered quietly into Aurel's ear and even though I couldn't hear what he was saying, I knew the words he was baiting him with.

"She's mine, and I won't give her up easily." With this, Kisten patted Aurel's shoulder and began to walk away. The gawkers began to awkwardly disperse, and Kisten turned to look to me where I stood. I understood his silent question, and, glancing back at Aurel one final time, I slid on my sunglasses as I jogged up to him. The vampire was standing still, his eyes locked on Kisten's back.

"Just doesn't know when to quit huh?" Kisten breathed, reaching to take my hand in his. I was surprised by the lack of pain and I looked down to notice that he had slipped on a leather glove, protecting me from the pain of this simple gesture. I looked back up to a soft smile on his face and he lifted my hand to kiss it.

"I don't want to hurt you every time." Kisten whispered, dropping our hands as we continued walking. I giggled softly, squeezing his hand in mine as he continued. "Sorry about Aurel, by the way. He's unlikely to give up for a while, given his persistence in the past."

"Because of you?" I offered and then I dropped my voice, uncertainty filling me. "Or because of me?"

"Well, I mean Aurel has never taken rejection well." Kisten shrugged, glancing at the other stores we walked past. His eyes lingered on The Dream for a moment, but he led us past, not stopping. "But I'm sure he thinks I'm trying to get revenge for what he did by taking you. And he's not completely wrong, just has things in the wrong order."

"You didn't even know about that until last night." I argued and Kisten shrugged again, his face showing his annoyance. It took me a moment to realize what he had fully said and I looked to him with surprise. "Wait, wrong order?"

"Why do you think I took you to The Dream, knowing Aurel would be there?" Kisten chuckled low in his throat, squeezing my hand tightly. "I almost didn't answer his call last night but I had wanted to rub you in his face. Finding out about Irida distracted me, but never changed my intention. Finding out he wanted you, well, that just made it that much better."

"Rub me in his face?" I asked darkly and Kisten looked down at me and, seeing my dark look, kissed my forehead gently. I stopped walking and he turned to face me, his loving smile on his face. "Did you know about Aurel and me?"

"No, not until you told me. I just wanted to show him I had moved on." Kisten sighed happily as he looked at me. My anger started to melt away under his loving gaze and he pulled me close as he finished. "Aurel insisted no one else would be willing to put up with me. I wanted to rub it in his face that someone would. He would've hated seeing me with anyone, but because of you, someone who also doesn't want him...

"Well, let's just say he-" Kisten stopped speaking as he looked up, seeing Aurel walking up to us quickly. The vampire's feet barely touched the ground and he was half-flying as he moved toward us. He sighed heavily, glancing around and his eyes rested on the bathrooms. He gently pushed me in their direction, and I turned to give him a confused look.

"He's not going to give up and I don't want you to be at the center of it again. This is more about us than you at this point." He smiled and I reluctantly went, looking back as Aurel reached Kisten. He looked as he was going to strike him, but Kisten merely smiled, not remotely intimidated by the vampire's aggression. I walked inside, disappearing before Aurel could notice.

I didn't have to use the toilet, so I merely took my sunglasses off and splashed some water on my face at the sink. I closed my eyes, sighing heavily at the thoughts that were rising up about Aurel and I did my best to push past them. I took in a deep breath and let it out shakily as I began to open my eyes.

A gloved hand appeared over my mouth and I immediately moved to retaliate until I felt a knife placed into my chest. I opened my eyes to see our suspect behind me, his dark brown eyes twisted with malice and his matted black hair peeking out from underneath his hood. He was still wearing the same outfit from Thursday night and he scowled at me in the mirror.

"Your Overseer has my Irida." He hissed, pressing the knife more into my skin. The knife was silver and he was aiming for my heart, so I knew he had taken me to be a shifter. As I was walking around with the Alpha, it was a reasonable assumption for him to make and I remained still, trying to think of my next move. While the silver itself was not a heavy concern, the knife was and I didn't want to risk him getting away if I defended myself, especially not with him so close.

"What do you want?" I breathed, doing my best to sound scared and worried. He pressed the knife into my skin more as he spoke again, the tip drawing a thin line of blood.

"I'm going to take you with me." He snarled, pulling us backwards towards a stall. "I've already left your Alpha a little present, letting him know I have his mate. Unless he brings me my Irida, I will kill you."

I gasped as we started the sink into the floor, failing to realize that he had drawn a Circle into the tiles. The door burst open and I saw Kisten and Aurel rush into the bathroom, not worried about what others thought. I reached up to my chest, tearing the locket housing my sister's soul from around my neck. I tossed it to Kisten before I disappeared completely into the bathroom floor and blacked out in the darkness.

19

When I came too, I was in a dark, dirty cage and surrounded by trees. I groaned as I sat up, trying to see if the witch was anywhere nearby. I couldn't see any signs of him in the darkness, so I tested the bars of my cage.

They were silver, as I expected, and a small test with my power proved that I could easily bend them. The culprit was so sure I was a shifter he didn't even bother to ensure the cage was sturdy, certain the silver would keep me from trying. Not wanting to give up my advantage, I left the bars alone and looked around the small clearing I was being kept in.

It was evident that he had been staying here for a short while, probably since Irida stopped herself from killing Justina. He knew it was a matter of time before we would be looking for him, so he was at least smart enough not to remain in the city. He had a small cooler and chair, with a dirty sleeping bag next to an equally dirty backpack. I couldn't see anything around me but trees, so I had no indication how far we were from the city or what direction the city would be in. There was barely any sunlight left in the sky above me, and I knew it had been at least a few hours since he had taken me from the bathroom.

"You're awake." I turned around as the witch appeared from the darkness of the woods, and he dropped to his hunches near the cage, glaring at me. I glared back, not even pretending to be afraid. He scoffed at this, producing a gun and he showed me the silver bullets in his other hand before loading it. "Behave."

I merely hissed at this as he walked away, watching him as he moved about his camp, retrieving something to drink from his cooler. He plopped down in his chair while downing the beverage, tossing the aluminum can into the trees near my cage. I saw it was beer and rolled my eyes, annoyed by this man's arrogance as he drank a second one. He clearly was too full of himself if he thought capturing me would get him what he wanted. Even if I had been Eve, no one was going to hand Irida to him: the only thing he was getting from anyone was a decent helping of death.

"Hmmmm," I looked up as the witch hummed and I nearly gagged from the look in his eyes. He was rubbing himself with the gun, and I knew what he was imagining. I growled at him, allowing my eyes to swirl with power and then pretending to be hurt by the cage. All I had to do was keep him near me long enough for Kisten and my team to find me. My locket would lead them straight to me, as my sister could only survive if the locket was near my heart and it was designed to find its way back to me.

"You're prettier than that stupid witch." I glared at him as he mentioned Justina and he smiled at my reaction, grabbing himself with his hand. "She should've just accepted the threesome with me and Irida and she never would've been hurt. Now I have to kill them both: a waste if you ask me, it'll be hard to find someone as easy to roll as Irida."

"You're disgusting." I spat and he stood up, overturning his chair and dropping the gun in his anger. He stomped towards me and reached through the bars, wrapping his hand around my throat. I instinctively reached to grab his wrist, but I realized there was no power in his grip. I chuckled, giving him a look of pity as I dropped my hand. "You're so fucking weak: now I understand why Irida thought you were human. You have to roll someone else to pull off a kill because there's no way you could ever dream of hurting someone."

"Shut up, bitch." He snarled, tightening his grip but it was a joke. I easily pushed his hand from around my neck and sat comfortably in my cage. He seemed ready to reach for me again, but instead he stood and went back to his overturned chair. He retrieved the gun and released the safety, shooting me in the cage. I gasped with pain as the bullet went through my left arm, and I held my hand to the wound. He laughed with triumph as he came back up to the cage and pointed the gun towards my head.

"Now, it is a matter of time before the silver kills you." He laughed, leaning close to my cage. "Hope your boyfriend is quick on his feet."

"You won't leave this forest alive." I swore and yelped with pain as he shot me again, this time catching my midsection. I was tempted to free myself from the cage and stomp him into the ground, but his shots were purposely missing anywhere vital. He was counting on the silver slowly killing me, which ironically would be his undoing.

Despite having the abilities of vampires, I was much easier to kill thanks to still being somewhat human, and major trauma to my heart or brain would easily render me lifeless. The silver would only slow my healing, not even weakening me as it would a vampire, so as long as he avoided a kill shot, I could recover from these injuries.

I forced myself to act as if my body was racked with pain as he gloated over me. He looked at the gun with a savage grin and for a moment I thought he was going to shoot me again for fun. It was obvious from his behavior he had never thought of using one before, which wasn't surprising. Most Supernaturals preferred their own abilities over human weapons and it was seen as weakness to rely on them. He placed the gun on the ground before he crouched in front of the cage again.

"Maybe I should have my fun with you before you die." He grabbed my chin, pulling my face closer to his. I spit in his face and it was his turn to growl as he backed away from me again. He wiped my saliva from his face, but he grinned at me, clearly liking this new idea. He carefully picked up the gun again and put it in my face. I was forced to comply as he pulled me out of the cage and stepped on my back, the gun still to my head. "Ruin you as a potential mate."

The witch started to slowly undo the back of my dress and I started to summon my power as he stroked my back with his free hand. He would kill me if he pulled the trigger, but there was no way I was going to let this sleaze have his way with me, the laws be damned. The air around us grew damp and heavy as my power grew and he paused, looking to the sky above us. Not seeing any clouds, he instantly connected the dots and he pressed the gun more into my head, forcing my face into the ground.

"Stop it." He hissed, and I flinched as he fired the gun next to my head. He leaned over me, shoving his foot into my back more.

The pain in my side increased from the added pressure and the blood began to flow more quickly as he spoke directly into my ear. "I don't care what you are, a silver bullet through your skull and heart will end you."

I hissed, but withdrew my power, the air becoming dry once again. The witch smiled above me, and he once again began to touch me with his free hand, taking his foot off my back. I clenched my teeth in the dirt, wanting nothing more than to throw this sorry excuse for a person off my back. There was a chance I could move faster than he could pull the trigger, but I knew there was no way I could dodge the bullet entirely.

I reached my boiling over point when the man's hand slid down to my posterior and I growled as he took his time fondling me, gripping and groping my flesh. When he started to slide his hand between my legs, I decided to make my move, not willing to let this man touch me anymore. I was Kisten's, and I would not allow this sorry excuse for a witch to defile me any longer.

I moved my hands underneath my chest, and ignoring the bullet hole in my arm, began to prop myself up. He pushed the gun into my skull more but upon noticing that he couldn't force me back to the ground, I heard him begin to pull the trigger.

Moving as fast as I could, I bucked my back and rolled away from the witch. I was slower than I was betting, my previous wounds slowing me down and I held my head as I began to bleed from the gunshot. The man stood, aiming the gun at me again, but he was distracted by a large noise approaching us.

A large blur shot from the trees behind him and pinned him to the ground, my locket in its mouth. The gun went off as it flew from his hand as he was forced into the dirt and Kisten placed his large paw on the witch's head, growling loudly. The rest of my team followed behind him with Lucius and Aurel also stepping into the space, the Overseer's presence alone intimidating in the growing darkness. As Brandon placed the barrel of his gun on the man's head, Kisten got off him, padding his way to me as he shifted.

"Raiven," His voice was full of relief and then turned to worry as he noticed the blood flowing between my fingers where I held my head. He was still wearing his red shirt and khakis and I smiled slightly at seeing him. Kisten ignored my smile and turned to call over his shoulder. "Justin, over here now."

Justin moved from behind Brandon to Kisten's side, revealing the Alpha's trauma kit as he holstered his gun. Kneeling in front of me, Justin began to address the wound to my arm as Kisten gingerly touched my side, lifting my dress to examine the wound there. He returned his attention to my face after instructing Justin how to temporarily dress the gunshot and he laid his hand on mine, gently moving it away from my head.

I closed my eyes as he examined the damage, the first tingles of feeling lightheaded hitting me. The bullet had grazed the side of my head, taking off the top of my right ear and Kisten growled as he moved to dress the wound.

"Kis..." I tried to whisper his name, but now that my adrenaline was fading, I suddenly found myself weak and struggling to speak. Kisten hushed me, placing my locket in my hand. I immediately felt my sister's concern and her voice burst into my mind as soon as I closed my fingers over the wood.

'Raiven, you idiot! What were you thinking allowing yourself to be bait? This bullshit isn't worth your life, dammit! You should've killed that excuse for a witch the minute he touched you!'

'Better me than Julia, and if I hadn't allowed him to take me, he would've just ran. We might have never caught him.' I reasoned, closing my eyes as I answered her. Kisten must've worried that I was passing out as he gently shook me. He sighed with relief when I opened my eyes, and I smiled softly at him again. I could still feel my sister's frustration and relief, but she didn't continue, instead fading away. I knew she was saving her words for later, once I was in a safer place.

"Can you stand?" Kisten's voice was soft and tender as he stood me up and I wobbled on my feet, dizzy from the blood loss. I fell into his arms and he scooped me up, careful to avoid putting unnecessary pressure on my wounded side and arm. I pressed my locket into my chest, insuring it was close to my heart once again.

Kisten adjusted me in his arms and turned as Brandon finished speaking to the witch.

"-sure the other Overseers would love a chance to punish you for your crimes and usually we'd pass you off to the first one you pissed off. But as you're in my jurisdiction now and harmed a member of my team," Brandon looked up to Lucius and the Overseer nodded. My boss's face turned savage as Julia pulled the man to his knees, keeping their guns pointed at him. The man hissed at Julia touching him, but she merely shoved her gun into his back more. Lucius stepped up to the witch, who, despite obviously being overwhelmed, looked into the vampire's eyes defiantly.

"Fuck you." He spat, spitting on the ground in front of Lucius. The vampire barely noticed: his eyes were locked on the sorry man before him. The witch spat again, clearly aiming for Lucius' clothing. "You think you're so much better than me just because you have longer fucking lives."

"No." Lucius' voice boomed through the trees, even though it was barely above a whisper. I heard the birds scatter into the night sky and other creatures scattered as well, sensing the killing intent in the air. "The woman you harmed is a witch too. The woman you used doesn't even live as long as you. I'm not better than you because I've lived longer."

"Lamias are good for rolling, weak minds and weak hearts." The witch gloated, clearly feeling no remorse for what he had done to Irida. "As far as that other bitch, mental casters are better off dead anyway."

"You are disgusting." Aurel offered, speaking in Lucius' place. The vampire walked up to the man, and very cleanly sliced off the man's arm with his newly shifted claws. I narrowed my eyes as the man screamed, gripping his new stump as his blood poured out. Aurel grinned savagely: due to his vampiric ability to change his hands to razor sharp claws, Lucius always gave Aurel the honor of doling out punishment to those who deserved it. Aurel licked the blood from his hand, his eyes aglow with excitement. "You will suffer for your crimes."

The man didn't respond, staring at his missing arm with horror and anguish. He looked up, and with anger in his eyes, spit in Lucius' direction again, soiling the vampire's shoes. At this, Lucius reacted, reaching down and lifting the man into the air by his head, the vampire's feet hovering above the ground. My team and Aurel stepped back as the air was flooded with electricity, small flashes of lightning visible in the air from the sudden change in charge. The man finally seemed to understand his position as he squirmed in the Overseer's grip, trying to free himself from Lucius.

"You, are simply trash." I buried my face in Kisten's chest as I heard Lucius crush the man's skull, the pop making me want to vomit. Lucius rarely was so violent, usually locking up anyone we caught into the Basement or giving the honor of execution to Aurel, but as the witch was a being without remorse, I understood why Lucius had wanted to do it himself. It wasn't like we could follow Division 11 protocol either: his ability to roll others made him too dangerous to attempt transport and it would've been equally dangerous to try to hold him for another Overseer to arrive.

Kisten watched calmly, only looking down to make sure I was still awake. His expression was as stoic as Lucius' had been and I wanted to reach up to touch his face but lacked the strength to try. I instead closed my eyes, burying my face against him again as he carried me out of the woods, and into the waiting ambulance. I chanced a glance as we walked by Aurel, but the vampire's expression was unreadable as we passed him.

Kisten placed me on the waiting gurney and climbed into the back beside me. He immediately started prepping my IV and I found the strength to move, using my free hand to touch his leg. He paused in his movements, taking a moment to touch me. His expression softened, and after laying a piece of gauze on my forehead, kissed me.

"It's okay, Rai." He whispered, placing my hand back on the gurney. He touched the gauze gingerly and I wished he would touch my skin, despite the pain it would cause. "You can sleep now."

His words were almost like a spell as I immediately began to pass out, my eyes closing and I drifted off to darkness as the ambulance drove off into the night.

20

I woke up in my own hospital room, for a moment wondering where I was. Crispin, Justina, Kisten and LeAlexende all stood in the room, talking in low voices on the other side of the curtain. At the sound of Justina's voice, I sat up, wincing as my body ached. I clumsily adjusted the hospital gown that I had been changed into and cleared my throat as I prepared to speak.

"Justina?" My voice was hoarse as I called out and the curtain was pulled aside. My friend's eyes welled with tears as she flung herself around me, crying openly.

"You're alright." She sobbed and I hugged her back tightly, my left arm still aching. I closed my eyes as I squeezed her, fighting my own tears as the three men joined us. "Raiven, I was so worried about you."

"That's what I should be saying," I retorted softly, pulling back and laying my hand on her stomach. "And the baby?"

"Just fine." She smiled and Crispin came up behind her, wrapping his arms around her midsection before kissing her neck. She shrugged him off and he backed away, still smiling. "Should've chosen a better father though."

"You wound me." Justina and I giggled at Crispin's theatrics and LeAlexende merely shook his head. I turned to face the Overseer as he lifted his phone, excusing himself out of the room. I turned to look at Kisten, who was still standing silently away from me. I leaned away from Justina and reached my hands out to him. Justina looked at me confused and then turned to Kisten.

Slowly, he stepped toward me and I pulled him closer, pressing my face into his coat. He stiffened under my touch, and I looked up to his face. His expression was unreadable, and I buried my face into him again.

"It's not your fault." I whispered, rubbing my face against him as I held him as close as the bed would allow. He relaxed a little at this, and he carefully placed his hands on my gown to return my gesture. I took it as a good sign, and pressed little kisses into his stomach. "I let him take me."

"He hurt you." Kisten spoke and I looked up to him again. His expression held all the pain and anguish he felt over me being hurt. He gently stroked my bandaged ear and I leaned into his hand, the bandages protecting me from the pain. "I should've been there."

"You were when it mattered." I stated, smiling up at him. "You, Brandon and Lucius saved me from the mess I put myself in, just as I knew you would."

"A feat I'd rather you not repeat." Lucius walked into the room, followed by Eve and LeAlexende. Kisten stepped away from me, and he moved next to Justina and Crispin at my feet as the Overseer walked in. I winced as he stood over me, fully expecting to be punished for my insubordination. "You disobeyed me twice during this case, Raiven."

"I know." I winced, and Eve smiled smugly, clearing enjoying the proceedings. She loved the idea of Lucius punishing me and was practically giddy as she waited to see what he would do. LeAlexende gave her a curious look, but soon looked away, seating himself into the chair behind Lucius. Lucius stood over me a moment and I slouched into the bed, waiting to see what he would do. To my astonishment, he placed his hand on my head and I looked up at him, surprised again by his smile.

"And yet, thanks to you, we were able to punish the one who hurt Justina and Irida." He sighed, releasing me. Eve turned to him, astonished by his words and her disappointment plain on her face. "I think the injuries you sustained are punishment enough."

"And Irida?" I ventured, my voice soft as I spoke. Lucius smiled again, looking at me softly. "Is she safe?"

"I spoke with Brandon and he gave me leave to release her back to her Overseer." I sighed with relief, leaning back into my bed. "Who has also agreed to help her rehabilitate. This experience and the revelation about her partner has left her mind...fragile."

I nodded, closing my eyes as I sank back into the bed. Irida had seemed like a gentle soul and after realizing what she had been used to do, it only made sense that she would have a mental break.

Lucius patted the sheets next to me, looking up to my other three companions.

"Since we're all here," he began and I opened my eyes again, wanting to watch the proceedings. "It seems there need to be some adjustments in my command."

Justina looked away sheepishly, but Lucius was far from upset. Instead, his eyes were lit up with mirth as he met Crispin's gaze. He glanced to Justina's midsection, before looking up to her face. "While I am excited for you both, Crispin has seniority here, so unfortunately Justina, you will have to relinquish your place as third."

"That's fine." Justina nodded, and her lover wrapped his arm around her, sneaking a kiss into her hair as Lucius turned his attention to Kisten. Kisten chanced a glance at Eve, before meeting his friend's gaze. Eve looked at him confused, before turning to look at Lucius' back, her anger starting to grow on her face. She looked like she wanted to say something, but Lucius ignored her as he kept his eyes locked on Kisten's. It was a long time before Lucius sighed and turned to me, smiling as well.

"If you would so like, Raiven, you may take her place." Lucius offered and I looked at him shocked. I was certain that I would've been relieved of Command as well, since Kisten was pursuing me as a mate. I turned to Kisten who smiled, touching my bed sheets near my hand. Lucius continued as I turned back to him incredulously. "Normally, you would take second, since being the Alpha's mate would give you more power over the pack. But I have a reliable second, despite his skirt chasing ways."

Eve looked as if she would lose her jaw to the floor and she passed her eyes between Kisten and me. Her surprise slowly turned back to anger, and then to malicious scheming as her eyes rested on me.

I knew that she was thinking what I also worried about: being Kisten's mate would cause a conflict of interest with my job and I would have to reveal my involvement with the Supernatural community. I gave her an equally challenging look, which took her back for a moment. Eve was also keeping her nature as a

Supernatural a secret and if she outed me, I would out her and I was more likely to keep my job, even if I lost my team.

Lucius seemed not to notice the silent fight Eve and I were having with our expressions and continued speaking, laying his hand on my bed again. "You are the next logical choice for third and a replacement I think Justina would agree with."

"Of course." Justina chimed, leaning forward from Crispin and smiling at Lucius. "Raiven is stronger than me anyway, she could've been third the moment she came. The only reason she's in this room is she allowed herself to be."

"Mostly true." I countered, but I said it with a smile as she leaned back, as if resting her case. Lucius turned to me for my answer and I looked down to my feet, flexing my toes under the bed spread. Moving up to third would pile more responsibility on me, and I worried that it would do more harm than good. Lucius had insisted that I join Command thanks to my age and power, but I only agreed to a low spot, considering the likelihood of the Hunters finding me. It was already dangerous enough that Lucius had agreed to protect me: the closer I was to him, the more likely it was that the Hunters would find him as well. I felt a hand on my thigh and looked over to Kisten, who was lightly encouraging me. I sighed heavily, already knowing what my answer had to be.

"I accept, Lucius." I spoke calmly and clearly, the air swirling in the room for a moment before settling back down. Lucius smiled broadly, stepping back as I accepted my new position. "I only hope we don't regret this."

"If Kisten doesn't, I certainly don't." Was the vampire's answer as he watched Kisten's hand on my leg and he turned to look at LeAlexende, who had watched the proceedings with semi interest. Upon noticing his friend's gaze on him, the Overseer shrugged, looking back down to his phone.

"This is your area, Luc. Your risks are your own." LeAlexende shook his head as he spoke, but both vampires were smiling as Lucius turned to walk away. Eve glared at Kisten and me once Lucius had past her, clearly not happy with this small victory Kisten had won behind her back. She looked ready to mouth something, but didn't, settling for a malicious grin as she followed her lover out of the room. Once she left, everyone in the room breathed a sigh of relief and I turned to LeAlexende, who was still sitting in his chair.

"How much longer are you going to stay?" I asked, and the vampire shrugged, not looking up to me.

"Until you're released, I guess." He replied dismissively, motioning toward Justina. "After all, I've spent most of this visit supervising sleeping women in hospital beds. Might as well see it to the end."

Crispin laughed openly at this while Justina looked away embarrassed, and I turned to Kisten as he chuckled slightly. LeAlexende smiled brightly, clearly pleased while he engrossed himself with his phone. I returned my gaze to Justina, just in time to see her looking at me. She was looking at Kisten's hand where it still sat on my thigh and she gestured toward it when she spoke.

"So, сестра⁸, when was I going to learn about this?" she inquired and Crispin held her close again, kissing her neck. I looked away, not really sure how to answer her. I had never shared my feelings toward Kisten with anyone, so her surprise was understandable. Considering how much I complained about Crispin, she probably would've thought I was still stuck on Mikael. At my lack of a response, she turned her attention to Kisten, who was still stroking my leg softly. "Well, Alpha? Since when have you decided to pursue my птица⁹, hmm?"

"How long have I wanted to, or when did I start?" Kisten asked softly and I turned to look up at him. He was looking at me lovingly and I hummed under his gaze, leaning into him as he pulled me against his coat once more. Justina lightly turned to LeAlexende when he chuckled and then returned her attention to us.

"I can imagine it started once I could no longer interject." She mused, placing her hand on her hips as she sized up Kisten. She then returned her attention to me and I shifted my eyes away again. From

---

⁸ Russian "Sister"
⁹ Russian "Raven"

the look in her eyes, I knew she wanted to lecture me. "And this is who you want, Raiven? Whom you've chosen despite everything?"

I nodded my head, looking into her eyes. She must've liked what she saw as she motioned her surrender, moving her hand to her still flat stomach. A small smile started on her face and I felt a strange ache in my chest.

"I guess I'm not one to judge, considering who I chose." Crispin gasped in fake surprise as she jabbed at him, but she didn't turn as she continued speaking. "I doubt you completely approve of him."

"I don't see the appeal." I admitted, and she chuckled at this, reaching up to touch her lover's face. Crispin leaned into her hand happily, nuzzling her palm. I watched their interaction with surprise: I had never seen Crispin act so sincere towards anyone since my arrival in The Capital. I shrugged, doing my best to smile. "But that's your choice at the end of the day."

"Well, there's some semblance of a good man underneath." She stroked his chin and the vampire hummed, wrapping both of his arms around her waist. I felt a tinge of pain in my chest at their display of affection, and from Kisten's tightened grip on me, I knew he felt it too. I looked up at him again and he was looking at the couple with an unreadable expression. I pressed a kiss into his coat, and he looked down to me again, a sad look in his eyes. The night we had together was both a blessing and a curse: it had given us a taste of what we could have and it made it harder to be without it.

Kisten released me, mumbling something about finding a nurse for tests as he left the room. He closed the door softly and I looked after him longingly, wishing I had said something before he left. Justina and Crispin soon excused themselves, citing their need to make Justina's next appointment before leaving me alone with LeAlexende. The Overseer was engrossed in his phone, or at least acting like it, so I leaned back into my bed, closing my eyes as I waited for Kisten to return.

21

Kisten soon returned with the nurse and they checked my vitals, changed my bandages, and disappeared again. I reached after Kisten as he turned, but he left without so much as a backwards glance and I sank back into my bed dejected. LeAlexende remained engrossed in his videos, a chuckle escaping him every now and then.

'Sis?' I reached out to her with my thoughts, gently resting my hand on the wood. Since the vampire was ignoring me, I took the chance to speak with her, wanting to check on her after all that had happened. I grew worried at her lack of a response, and I gripped the locket tighter as I reached out again. 'Sis?!'

'Hush...I'm still here.' She reprimanded, and I breathed a heavy sigh of relief as I relaxed my grip. She was struggling to stay awake, and her voice sounded far and distant. 'Good to see...that you're up.'

'Are you alright?' I queried, and she took her time responding, as if it were difficult to find the strength.

'I'll live...for now. Separating me from you was...reckless...and stupid.' She berated and I winced under her harsh words. 'I know...you were thinking on your feet...and at least...you didn't run away...'

'I'm sorry.' I gripped the wood tightly again, my heart beginning to pound as I considered the worst. Without my life energy to feed on, it only made sense that the locket would have fed on hers. My impromptu plan had cost me valuable time with my sister, time I could never get back.

'You...don't have much longer...to make your choice, sis.' Tears welled up in my eyes at her calling me sis. She was rarely so informal with me, usually using my current name rather than a term of endearment. Given our history it was understandable, but I couldn't help enjoying when she showed how much she still cared. 'I will...rest as much as possible...and only check on you when...I'm needed. Sound... fair?'

'*Alright.*' I conceded, dropping my hand as I closed my eyes to the bright white lights. '*Good night.*'

'*Goodnight, Raiven.*' As my sister faded, I took a deep breath, letting it out shakily. I felt as if my chest would collapse in on itself from the thought of losing my sister. I didn't want to consider the idea of being without her but I also didn't want her to fade away. If I didn't return her to her body, her essence would simply fade into the ether and it would be as if she never existed.

I was jolted from my thoughts and opened my eyes to see LeAlexende standing, drawing the curtain to hide me from whomever was walking in the door. I froze in the bed, not sure who could have arrived to give LeAlexende such a reaction.

"I do believe you should not be here." The Overseer's tone was calm and he remained standing, his shadow projecting onto the screen that separated us. The other party spoke and my heart froze as soon as I recognized the voice.

"Now I'm not even allowed to visit her?" Aurel insisted, and he was trying to walk past the Overseer but LeAlexende was insistent as well. He blocked Aurel's movements, keeping him away from the bed.

"Even if you were allowed, she is sleeping." The Overseer lied smoothly, and I closed my eyes, trying to steady my heartbeat in case Aurel managed to move aside the curtain. "But I do believe you are not allowed near her regardless, since Lucius told me you have fed recently."

"That was days ago." Aurel whined and I rolled my eyes behind their lids. Even though he knew the rules, Aurel was willing to use any excuse to be near me, especially with Kisten away from my side. LeAlexende must've sensed the ulterior motive as well, as he dropped his voice as he spoke.

"She is injured, she is likely to lose control if she smells fresh blood. The only living allowed in her room is her doctor." The Overseer purposely avoided saying Kisten's name or mentioning that Justina had been here earlier, and Aurel fell right into the trap, scoffing as he tried to push past again.

"If she can stand Kisten, she can stand me." I heard him walk to my curtain and I held my breath as I waited to see what would happen. The door opened again and from the shifting energies in the air, I knew it was Kisten.

"Aurel," he said his name plainly, walking past him. Kisten gently pulled the curtain back, placing the results of my blood work on my screen. He stepped back to the other side, separating me from their eyes once more and I took the chance to open my eyes slightly. "You're not supposed to be here. If you want to talk to Raiven, wait your seven days or-"

"Shut up." The vampire hissed and the power in the air shifted again as Aurel grew angry. Kisten remained calm, placing his tablet down before crossing his arms where he stood. "You have no say in this."

"Considering I'm her doctor right now, I do." Kisten replied coolly, but I could feel his power beginning to rise as he grew angry. "Right now, I couldn't care less about your issue with me. Raiven is still recovering and I'm keeping my distance as well to prevent her blood lust from taking over. So, wait your last few days and then come see her if you want to talk to her that badly."

"You can't order me to do anything. You are not my Overseer." Aurel sounded as if he meant to force his way to me, but Kisten refused to move, blocking the vampire's access. LeAlexende sat down in his chair loudly, his power beginning to fill the room, overwhelming both Aurel's and Kisten's.

"I don't know what your problem is, 6th." The Overseer threatened, using Aurel's rank rather than his name to address him. I heard the two men turn to the vampire and from what I could see of their shadows, LeAlexende was looking at his phone again. "But you will not threaten the safety of my charge. I am responsible for Raiven as long as she remains here.

"So, you can leave," the vampire paused, and I could feel his annoyance in the air, a slight wind blowing through the room despite the window next to me being closed. "And wait until the end of your seven days or I will escort you out, and I will make sure Luc knows how willing you are to break his rules."

Aurel seemed to take LeAlexende's threat to heart, as I soon heard him walk out the room, slamming the door behind him. The air returned to normal as LeAlexende relaxed and Kisten sighed heavily, running his hand through his hair.

"Competition?" LeAlexende asked quietly, and Kisten scoffed, dropping his hand. He appeared to glance at the shut door, considering his answer.

"More like obsession. You know how Aurel can be when he wants something."

"Hmmm, more like he still hasn't gotten over you." The Overseer offered and Kisten remained silent. I saw his hand on the curtain again and closed my eyes as he pulled it back to look at me. I steadied my breathing to mimic sleep, and he sighed again, moving the curtain back to separate us.

"That too, but to be honest, I haven't gotten over it either." He admitted, sitting down in the chair across from LeAlexende. He slouched in the chair, clearly worn out from his labor. Even though I was his main concern, Kisten was on shift today, and was only checking on me in between his other patients. He let out a heavy sigh, almost groaning as he continued speaking. "He is not going to let me court her without a fight."

"Well, does your courtship have anything to do with him?"

"No." Kisten answered, and then he sat up, holding his hands in front of his lap. The pair remained silent for a moment and then Kisten spoke softly. "I love Raiven. I want her because of that, not to get back at him for what he did. But...

"I'll admit, I have been flaunting it in his face, and that was before I knew he wanted her." Kisten admitted, leaning back in his chair, slouching as his feet slid across the floor. "I enjoy showing him that I have what he wanted. That he was wrong about me and on top of that, I beat him at something. He thought he could have her easily and I just..."

Kisten made a grabbing motion with his hands, cupping them as if he were holding a delicate flower. His voice was soft and loving and my chest ached with his words. "Snatched her away. And now she's going to be mine, not his."

"So?" The Overseer offered, putting his phone down as he looked up to meet Kisten's gaze. I desperately wished I could see my lover's face, but I remained silent, keeping my façade as they spoke. "Are you going to stop pursuing her again? Are you going to let Aurel have his way?"

"No. Never." Kisten's response was immediate, and I smiled at his words, my heart pounding. The Alpha sat up again, his posture determined. "I...stopped myself once from pursuing her because I thought it would be better for both of us. I was wrong. I won't allow him to get in my way."

"Good to see you still have some fighting spirit. A part of me worried you had lost it." LeAlexende chuckled, slouching in his seat and looking back to his phone. Kisten chuckled as well, standing from his seat.

"Never, Alex. I'm still here to save you when you need it." The Overseer laughed as Kisten left and we were left in silence again. I almost sat up, wanting to ask the Overseer about Kisten's words, but decided against it, laying back on the bed.

"How long are you going to stay quiet?" LeAlexende's voice startled me, and I jumped slightly as he pulled back the curtain, smiling at me knowingly. I shrugged, closing my eyes.

"Well, I figured I shouldn't let Aurel find out you were lying." I retorted and LeAlexende chuckled, leaning against the wall. I chanced a glance at the Overseer, my eyes drifting to the closed door to my room. "And well, it didn't feel like I should interrupt your conversation with Kisten."

"Well, do you have anything to add, Raiven?" The Overseer's gaze betrayed his bright smile and I frowned, returning my eyes to the ceiling.

"I don't like being in the middle of their issue." I admitted, closing my eyes as I sighed. "I know they have their issues and I'm not saying Kisten's wrong, but I don't like him using me to get back at Aurel.

"But... Aurel is really the one making it a huge problem, because he wanted me for his harem." I sighed, looking over to LeAlexende again. The Overseer hadn't moved and was still watching me with the same expression and my frown deepened. "I should've told him long before now that I didn't feel that way about him, but honestly at this point I don't think it would've made a difference."

"Want an outsider's opinion?" The vampire offered and I nodded, waiting for him to speak. LeAlexende sighed, moving next to the bed and taking my hand. He squeezed it slightly, stroking my skin before speaking. "Aurel would've made it about him and Kisten even if Kisten had chosen someone else. He may say he accepts Kisten's decision but he never will, no more than he'll ever accept yours. Would you like to know exactly what Aurel told Kisten when Kisten turned him down?"

I nodded again and the vampire squeezed my hand again, releasing me as he leaned against the bed, facing away from me. His voice was soft when he resumed speaking.

"Kisten left The Capital that night and came to me in the Southern Grove." I couldn't help the shocked look on my face and LeAlexende chuckled, sensing my surprise despite not seeing my face. "I was shocked too, until he told me what happened. Aurel had told him that Lucius kept him bound via the Oath because no one else would ever risk being with someone like him. That he was a bound animal, only to be used by its master and had no other value than that use."

I was stunned into silence. I had never imagined Aurel could say something like that: he could be harsh with his words when he was upset, but not only had he tried to demean Kisten, he went as far as to accuse Lucius of being like Mater Vitae. My hands curled into fists at my anger and LeAlexende glanced back at me, his expression blank.

"Of course, when I brought Kisten back, I told Lucius what I had been told." The vampire turned away from me again, his voice holding back his obvious anger at the memory. "Aurel was dropped from third to sixth then, but Lucius wouldn't get rid of him thanks to his power. I warned him then, Aurel would only become more of an issue as time went on."

"I'm guessing Lucius said he'll deal with it then?" I offered and LeAlexende laughed, completely turning to face me again.

"You have gotten a good grip on him in your short time here." The Overseer chuckled and I couldn't help but smile back. LeAlexende took my hand again, his eyes boring deep into mine as he spoke. "I'll tell you the same thing I told him: be wary of Aurel. He only does whatever he thinks will get him his way."

"I will, Alex. Thank you." With this, he released me and returned to his seat, resuming his video surfing on his phone. I sighed deeply, reflecting on what LeAlexende had told me. Kisten's desire to get back at Aurel made more sense to me now, but I still didn't enjoy being at the center of their issues.

'*What would Aurel have said to me to get me to choose him?*' I wondered silently, and then I gripped the sheets tightly. '*What will he say?*'

I shook my head to try to free myself of these thoughts. I rolled on my side, wincing from the pain and closed my eyes, hoping to sleep away my turmoil.

22

I sat on my couch in the warm afternoon, flipping through channels as my cats lounged around me. Brandon had visited me while I was in the hospital and insisted that I stay home for a few days. The team was getting ready to fly out on a new case, but he was adamant that they would call me if I was needed.

I accepted his demand easily: I didn't really want to get back to work so soon. It wasn't the first time I had ever been injured on a case, and I never felt like jumping back in afterwards. I almost convinced myself to tell Brandon the truth but stopped myself. I knew I would have to speak with the Director first, and it would ultimately be his decision as to what happened next.

Kisten released me the day after Brandon's visit and took me home, my car having already been driven from The Dream for me. My two cats were excited to see me after the days I had been gone and I was equally happy to see them, dropping immediately to pet them. Kisten had left silently after seeing me inside, not giving me the chance to say goodbye as he closed my front door behind him.

I hadn't heard a word from him in the past day, and a pit began to form in my stomach as I checked my phone for the millionth time. I wasn't surprised he hadn't come by, but I had expected at least a phone call or a message. My thoughts turned to Eve's mischievous smile at the hospital and Aurel's insistent visit shortly after, causing me to groan loudly into the pillow.

"He won't give up." I tried to reason with myself, laying down as I settled on my usual cartoons. I almost expected my sister to respond, but she remained withdrawn. She hadn't spoken to me since the hospital and if it wasn't for her occasional presence to see how I was doing, I would've thought she had truly faded completely. As she had pointed out, eventually I would have to make my decision: to allow her soul to fade into obscurity, or to give her peace by returning it to her body.

The pit in my stomach increased with these thoughts and I groaned out loud, causing my cats to stand up and shift their positions, clearly not wanting to deal with my anguish. I tried my best to pay attention to the colorful characters on my screen, but my own thoughts kept me from paying much attention to the lighthearted cartoon.

A sudden knock at the front door made my heart race and I nearly ran to the door, about to throw it open when I forced myself to pause. Taking a deep breath, I glanced out the peephole, wanting to make sure it was Kisten before I threw myself into the arms of a stranger. I had nearly done it earlier with another delivery man, who was merely dropping off my monthly order of food for my cats. He was clearly taken aback as I flung the door open and I had been more than embarrassed as I signed for the box.

It was Aurel, the vampire leaning on my porch railing as he waited. My heart sank again, but not only from disappointment. Aurel's insistence that I choose him over Kisten was truly making me despise him and I regretted agreeing to be friends more and more. LeAlexende's warning the hospital returned and my heart began to pound.

He knocked on the door again and I merely leaned against it, wishing for him to go away. I noticed his shadow against my curtained window, and I knew he was trying to see if I was in my living room.

'I'm sleeping, go away. I don't want to see you.' I thought as he knocked a third time, his patience decreasing with his pounding. I considered locking myself up in my room in case he tried to force my door open, but I forced myself to remain still, lest he heard me walk away. I wanted to look out the peephole again but was too afraid I'd see him trying to look in for me.

"I know you're there Raiven!" He finally growled and I stiffened, too scared to breathe. I felt my sister's presence rise, but she remained silent as we both waited to see what the vampire would do. He pounded on the door again and I had to cover my mouth to hide the sound that tried to escape me. "I just want to talk!"

'I'd hate to see what he'd do... if he wanted to do more than talk.' My sister sneered and I nodded silently, jumping again as he continued pounding on my door. I slowly began to back away as I saw my door frame move with his pounding. The last thing I wanted was to face Aurel if things got physical, but I knew I would have no choice if he broke down my door.

"Raiven, please." His voice was soft now and I could hear him lean against the door. I scoffed: now he wanted to plead with me as if he had not just been pounding against my door like an angry ex? "I just... I just want to talk to you without him around."

After a moment of silence, I heard him place something on the doorstep and walk away. He paused for a moment at the end of the porch, presumably turning back to look at my door but he soon continued walking and I breathed a sigh of relief as his car started in my driveway. I waited until I could no longer hear his motor as he drove off down the street before I opened the door, seeing a small package on my doormat. There was no note attached and I looked at it cautiously as I picked it up and closed my front door.

I held the package with disgust, angry that Aurel would even consider leaving me a gift after what he had done. Knowing him, it was probably a piece from his jewelry collection, trying to show me that he really cared about me but I didn't want it. It was nothing more than a trap and I was determined to throw it away as I walked back into my home. I was in no way prepared for the solid mass I ran into as I stepped into my kitchen.

"Distracted?" I nearly flung the package from my hands as I threw my arms around Kisten. My side door was open, and my cats pawed at the screen door, wanting the freedom of outside as I embraced my love. Kisten pulled me closer to him, planting soft kisses into my hair. "It almost seems like you missed me."

"Of course I did." I breathed, resting my chin against his chest as I looked up at him. Kisten smiled down at me, and I leaned up for a kiss, him meeting me halfway. I almost moaned at the searing pain of our lips slanting across each other, but I had missed kissing him more than anything.

Kisten pulled back before I could deepen the kiss and stepped away, turning around to close my side door. I placed Aurel's package on the counter as I walked up behind him, unable to keep my hands off my Alpha.

"How did you get here?"

"I ran." He said and I turned him around, trying to measure if he was joking. He still had the same smile on his face as he stroked my scarred face down to my injured earlobe. I had insisted he remove the bandage before releasing me and I was shocked by how normal it still looked. The bullet had taken off a decent amount but it was still less than I expected, something Kisten amounted to it also grazing my face as I had moved, therefore slowing it down ever so slightly. I leaned into his painful touch, pressing his hand against my face and I closed my eyes as he continued. "I was talking with Lucius."

"About?" I asked, my eyes still closed as I took in him being here with me. Kisten chuckled and I lazily opened my eyes to see his grin.

"Us." Kisten stated, pulling me into another embrace. He kissed my ear and I sighed happily despite the burning pain. "There are more steps to courtship, and I was going through them with Lucius, including when he would release the Oath."

"Hmm." I hummed in agreement, burying my head into his chest. His shirt smelled heavily of sweat even though the fabric was dry, so I knew he ran from the Landing in animal form. He pressed more kisses into my hair, before looking away from me and his grip on me suddenly tightened. I followed his gaze to the package on my counter, still wrapped and unopened.

"Who's that from?" He asked, and I froze, not wanting to tell him Aurel had been here. He looked at me darkly as my heart pounded and I kept my gaze away from him. His voice was dark and full of suspicion as he spoke again, this time speaking directly against my skin. "Raiven, who is that from?"

"It's fro-" I barely got a word out before Kisten pinned me to my counter, pushing his body into mine. I gasped at the sudden movement, wrapping my arms around Kisten's neck as he lifted me on the marble and began to assault my neck, burning my skin with his licking and biting. I moaned openly at his assault and he wrapped one of his arms around me, sliding my groin into his as he leaned over me, undoing the buttons of my shirt with his free hand. He growled into my skin and I moaned for him, loving every second of this punishment.

"Don't accept gifts from him." He commanded, sliding his hand up my stomach once the fabric fell open. I clung to him uselessly, only able to nod at his command. He licked up my collarbone, a trail of pain following his sandpaper tongue. "I don't care if they pile up on your doorstep. I don't want you to touch them. Let me take care of them."

"Yes..." I moaned and Kisten paused in his torture, pulling back slightly to look at my face. My eyes fluttered open as I breathed heavily, my body full of pain and my desire for him. His eyes were swirling, and he growled above me, the sound causing my midsection to clench with promised pleasure and pain.

"Good." With no small ceremony, Kisten lifted me off the counter and over his shoulder, jolting me from my stupor. I heard him scrape the package into the trash before carrying me out of the kitchen, and I knew his intentions before we reached my bedroom. He tossed me on the bed, climbing on top of me before I could even finish bouncing from the impact. His mouth was already back on my neck and I wrapped my legs around his waist, pulling him closer to me. As I surrendered to the painful pleasure of his touch, I knew I had chosen correctly.

23

LeAlexende lounged on the train station bench, placing his phone down next to him. It seemed the Overseer had exhausted everything he wanted to do, and he slouched, running his hand through his blond hair. He pulled a few strands in front of his face, grunting before pushing them back with the rest. His expression was pensive and he glanced up towards the dark night sky.

"Sorry I'm late." LeAlexende looked down to see Lucius walking towards him alone, finally without Eve tailing behind him. He sat next to him on the bench, and for a moment, the two friends took in the empty station devoid of life. The silence was deafening: no wind to blow around the debris and trash, no insects to sing their nightly song. A perfect setting for two undead beings to speak.

"Sorry that your visit was disrupted like this. It was...not ideal." Lucius was first to break the silence, slouching to match LeAlexende. He sighed heavily, and LeAlexende snorted, closing his eyes.

"This is your territory: I didn't expect a peaceful visit. Even without Raiven's case, you keep too many dangerous people around." LeAlexende sighed, picking himself up and sitting properly on the bench. A train flew by in the quiet night, interrupting the silence with its noise. LeAlexende watched it with semi-interest as it passed, the lights a blur as it flew by. It left as quickly as it came, bringing with it the façade of life as the wind of its passing moved his hair in its wake. LeAlexende lifted his hand to his hair again as he spoke. "It's more than enough that I got to see you."

"What did you come for? You don't usually visit without warning." Lucius asked, chancing a glance at his friend. LeAlexende didn't answer at first, keeping his gaze on the darkness the train had ventured into. Lucius opened his mouth to speak again, but decided against it, waiting patiently for his friend.

"Basina...is dead." LeAlexende closed his eyes, a pained expression on his face. Lucius' eyes widened in surprise and he stammered to answer.

"But...she-"

"They got her. I heard it from her second." LeAlexende continued, ignoring Lucius' surprise. His expression was heavy and it was clear the news was difficult for him as well. "With her gone, we're the last high ranking First left."

"Just less than half of the original thirteen now." Lucius sighed, and LeAlexende nodded, his blond hair rippling as his fingers passed through. In a moment, his hair turned white as fresh snow and his purple eyes had almost deepened to black. Lucius was unsurprised by this change and merely looked on as LeAlexende stood. His face and form also seemed more feminine somehow, but his voice sounded the same when he spoke.

"Lucius, I'm the only one left who truly remembers and with Basina gone, I'm the last of the siblings. It's only a matter of time now." LeAlexende's voice was barely above a whisper and Lucius looked as if he was about to argue. He stopped however, as LeAlexende raised his hand in front of Lucius. "There needs to be someone else who remembers."

"Alex, don't do this. It'll weaken you too much. If he is after you, you need all of your strength." Lucius pleaded, even as he knelt underneath LeAlexende's hand. It was obvious he didn't want to, but it was almost as if he was being forced to comply. "Let me go get a memory device, that should suffice-"

"No, Luc. We need to do this the old way and you're the only person I trust." LeAlexende insisted, and Lucius was crestfallen at his friend's insistence. "You need to feel my memories. You need to know the truth."

Lucius nodded, and LeAlexende smiled a sad smile as he brought his wrist to his mouth. He pierced his own skin with his fangs and allowed his blood to drip over Lucius' face. His purple eyes began to glow and the white hair swirled in the wind his power had called forth.

"Enkidu, son of Damuzi," LeAlexende used Lucius' human name, causing Lucius' power to come forth on its own. Lightning flashed in the sky above the pair, a storm beginning to form over the train station. "Accept the blood of Latinius and allow my memories to be yours."

With this, Lucius opened his mouth, allowing the blood of his friend and fellow Overseer to flow into him. The storm above them grew in turmoil and LeAlexende lifted his eyes up from Lucius. His eyes seemed to meet mine as the lightning flashed and I woke up as the thunder crashed above the pair.

It was dark in my room after the flash, and I could hear Kisten sleeping peacefully next to me. I carefully stood and walked to my window, seeing the brewing storm on the horizon. I could feel my sister's presence and without words, I knew she was thinking the same as me.

"What was that..." I wondered aloud, and a thought flashed through my mind, my sister pushing the concept to me. "Necromancy..."

Despite my necromancy saving me from being turned into a vampire, it was not an ability I had ever used. I had only used it once in my long life and that was when my sister died. Mater Vitae had forbidden me from ever using it and after I left, I never felt the need.

Necromancers were extremely rare among humans, to the point most never knew they were one unless they accidentally called upon the power. Thanks to their power to raise the dead, they were always in demand, and we would sometimes call upon one to help with our investigations.

"That's impossible, sis. Necromancy doesn't work on vampires." I rebutted and she left, not arguing with me. I continued looking at the still growing storm, still trying to process what had happened and what I had seen. Another First was dead: that's why LeAlexende had come to visit without warning. More than half of the First were now gone and that meant the Hunters would soon be closing in on the few who remained. I gripped myself tightly, my room briefly filling with light as the lightning flashed again.

'Don't...' I was surprised by my sister's voice and I gripped the locket as she came back, her frustration obvious. I glanced to the floor, afraid to see my own reflection in the glass. *'Don't you run this time. Don't you give this...up out of fear.'*

"I..." I started to dispute her assumption but I stopped myself. I always ran when I knew the Hunters getting close and I felt the familiar urge to flee now. I turned to look at Kisten, who was still sleeping peacefully on my bed. My heart pounded as I looked at him and I gazed back to the storm that was growing ever closer.

LeAlexende had been worried enough that he had wanted to share his memories and power with Lucius and my Overseer was known for his habit of taking risks. Staying with him meant putting everyone in The Capital in danger but leaving him meant losing Kisten.

I sighed heavily, pulling myself away from the window and back to the bed. Kisten rolled over to me, draping his arm across my waist as I sat down. I couldn't help my smile as I laid down, gingerly touching his face with my fingertips. Kisten sighed happily in his sleep, leaning into my touch as my fingers ached with pain. I gripped my sister's locket as I closed my eyes.

'Don't worry.' I assured her, breathing deeply as she faded away. *'I won't.'*

Preview of Book 2:

To Spot a Leopard

1

I leaned against the pier, looking out over the ocean as the sea breeze blew through my hair and shirt. I didn't visit the ocean very often, and as I looked over the blue expanse, I was filled with a longing for a home I barely remembered. Somewhere, across all that water, was my first home and where my sister's body was buried. I held her locket in my hand, trying to encourage her to speak, but the wood remained hard and silent.

Six months ago, my best friend Justina had been injured by an insane witch, who was using his lamia girlfriend to kill anyone who offended him. I allowed myself to be captured by him and had given my locket to Kisten, the local Alpha, to allow him to find me. I suffered the consequences of my rash decision, including losing part of my right ear. The locket had been dependent on my sister's soul power while it was separated from me, and the result left my sister with barely enough soul to hold on.

"Are you alright, *Rabe*[10]?" I turned to see Kisten, who was walking up to me, using one of his many pet names for me. The Alpha was wearing a sheer white shirt, the fabric hanging loosely around him as it blew in the wind. His shorts also flapped in the breeze and I couldn't help my excitement as he grew closer. I turned around completely as he reached me, a bright smile gracing my face.

"I am now." I smiled, leaning up to kiss him as he wrapped his arms around my waist. My mouth exploded with the familiar pain as our lips touched and I ignored it as I stroked his face with my gloved hands. Kisten pulled up from me, his eyes bright with his smile as he pulled me closer.

"I'm glad." He glanced down to my collarbone, where his necklace sat around my neck. Kisten was pursuing me as his Beta, and the necklace was a part of the courtship process, essentially marking me as his. From what I had experienced so far, most of the

---

[10] German "Raven"

process included many gifts, including clothing I had to wear at certain times symbolizing his continued pursuit.

It was all to build to a declaration, asking me to be his mate in public and me accepting. I was both excited and scared of that moment: it would be then that I would have to reveal my relationship with Kisten to my job and run the risk of losing it. Only the Director knew of me being more than human and I had to maintain my distance from the Supernatural community in order to avoid a conflict of interest. Agreeing to be Kisten's mate would no longer allow me to keep that distance, and it would be up to the Director what happened next.

"Are you excited for tomorrow?" Kisten inquired, his words pulling me from my thoughts as he leaned next to me. I followed his gaze down to the beach, where people moved to and fro preparing for the wedding. It would be the union of Arkrian and Shannon, a snake shifter from Kisten's pack and my boss' daughter. I shrugged, looking away.

"As much as I can be." I muttered, closing my eyes as I enjoyed the breeze. Kisten hummed, placing his arm around my waist. I leaned into him as he stood, sighing heavily. "My whole team is going to be there, so I'm not particularly excited about them hearing your declaration."

"They were going to find out eventually." He shrugged, laying a kiss on my braids. I sighed again: he was right as usual, but it didn't erase the worry in my chest. Kisten pulled away from me and started to lead me down the pier. "C'mon, we need to find the happy couple."

As Arkrian's Alpha, Kisten had an important role to play in the ceremony: apparently it was tradition for Alphas to preside over the event, officially joining the new couple. After learning I was to be Kisten's Beta, Shannon offered me a spot as one of the bridesmaids, but I refused, not wanting to intrude on her special day.

The ceremony was already something unique in its own right and an upcoming trend in mixed marriages: similar to what her brother had done, Shannon wanted to mix human traditions with shifter traditions. Her take on what traditions to use had upset her father somewhat, as Brandon wasn't exactly fond of shifters, but he conceded in the end.

"Raiven!" Shannon ran up to me, a giddy expression on her face as she ran up the pier. Kisten released me as we collided, the petite girl nearly knocking me over. Shannon was a perfect copy of her late mother: long blond hair, bright brown eyes, a petite hourglass figure, and the attitude of someone twice her height. There wasn't much that could deter her from having her way and that included her future husband.

Her fiancé walked up to us slowly, shaking his head at Shannon's behavior. Arkrian was much more stoic that his bride-to-be: in a lot of ways he reminded me of Kisten. He wore a cool head on his shoulders, polite to a fault, but also a fighter for what he wanted. He was the Omega to Kisten's Alpha and next to take Kisten's place, an honor he had earned on more than one occasion.

"Shannon," Arkrian sighed as he reached us, pausing a moment to greet Kisten. His dark brown waves blew in the wind, and he took a moment to brush them from his face. "Don't jump on Raiven like that."

"Oh hush, Ark. Raiven can easily catch me." As if to prove her point, Shannon jumped up on me, wrapping her legs around my waist. I moved my arms to hold her, my eyes swirling as I summoned my power. Being part undead had its advantages, such as having a degree of inhuman strength and I carried Shannon easily. Kisten laughed as Arkrian shook his head and I gently put the girl down on the pier. Arkrian moved as if to apologize, but I stopped him with a smile.

"Don't bother," I beamed, moving next to Kisten as Shannon returned to Arkrian's side. "We both know it won't do any good."

"That's...true." Arkrian conceded, kissing his bride's cheek. She glowed at the gesture and leaned into him, clearly happy and excited. My chest hurt at their display of affection, but I kept the smile on my face while Arkrian questioned Kisten about the ceremony.

Despite my future at his side, Kisten was still bound to Lucius and Eve via the Oath: a promise of loyalty that kept others from touching him intimately. Even the slightest display of affection would cause me intense pain, and I rarely got to experience the intimacy others took for granted. Kisten had promised that the Oath would be released at some point during the courtship, as he had to be released from it before I could become his mate. However, he never told me when, and the longer I had to wait, the more unbearable it became to deal with.

"Well, Shannon wants to double check the preparations for tomorrow with the hotel, and then we still need to pick up some things." Arkrian went on, and I returned my attention to him. "We'll see you both at the dinner tonight?"

"Of course, *der Welpe*[11]." Kisten smiled and we watched as they walked up the pier, both hand in hand. Kisten looked down to me, and I must've held my longing on my face, as he grabbed my hand. The gloves I wore had been a courting gift, and he lifted my hand to his mouth, kissing the fabric.

"Soon enough." He promised, his chartreuse eyes bright with his love for me. Despite the ache in my chest, I smiled back, closing my eyes.

"I know, Kisten." I stroked his face with my free hand, leaning into his embrace again as he buried his face into my neck. I held his head against me, loving the feel of him. "I can't wait."

"We could get joined here too." He offered and I chuckled, tapping him playfully. "It would be quite the romantic wedding."

"You really want to copy them?" It was his turn to laugh as Kisten lifted me into the air, setting me on the lip of the pier. He pressed his face into my midsection, taking in the scent of me that he enjoyed so much. I rested my hand on his head, lightly stroking his hair. "Never took you as one to enjoy the beach."

"I can't say I'm completely fond." He admitted, looking out towards the sea. A sad look crossed his face before disappearing. "Crossing the Atlantic in the 1800s is not as luxurious as it is now."

"I'd imagine not." I agreed, looking back over the ocean. I could see the faint shadow of a ship on the horizon, and I watched as

[11] German "Pup"

it drifted further along the expanse of blue. I turned back to see Kisten looking up at me, his expression quizzical.

"Now that I think about it," he started, his eyes meeting mine. "You've never told me where you came from. You had to cross the sea at some point."

I shrugged, not answering his question as I looked back over the water, holding my locket through my shirt. Kisten watched my hand, not pressing me for an answer. After the ordeal with the witch, I confided in Kisten, making him the only person alive who knew the truth about my sister and the locket. Most assumed it was a collar from my time with Mater Vitae, not understanding the true value it held to me. Kisten had insisted he would help me if I wanted to give my sister peace, but it still wasn't something I was ready to do.

'Raiven...' I nearly jumped as I finally heard her voice, soft and barely above a whisper. She must've felt me thinking about her and it was probably taking all her strength to reach out to me.

"Sis?" I spoke quietly, and Kisten looked up to me, concern flashing across his features. He reached to touch my locket as well, allowing him to hear her voice as she continued, the strain obvious in her tone.

'Just...checking in. Harder to stay awake now.' She sounded far away and my heart ached as she continued to speak. 'Kisten, keep taking care...of her.'

"Of course." He smiled and I felt the warmth fade as my sister drifted away again. His hand slowly slid away as I released the locket, tears forming in my eyes.

"She's going to fade soon." I lamented, my voice full of the tears I refused to let flow. "I don't have much time with her left."

"What do you want to do?" I met his gaze as he spoke, his voice full of concern. I leapt down from my perch, pulling him into a tight hug as I held back my tears. I shook my head against him and he tightened his grip on me, pressing comforting kisses into my hair.

"I don't know." I admitted, speaking into his chest. "I...I don't know."

"C'mon," he coaxed, gently pulling away from me. His hand caressed my face, the gentle act marred by the pain it caused. "We've got some time before dinner. Let's walk around for a bit."

As Kisten gently led me down the pier, I chanced one last glance at the ocean. It gently lapped in my direction, as if reminding me that I would one day have to cross it again. I forced myself to look away, squeezing my partner's hand tightly.

Yasmina Iro

Author Bio

When it comes to traveling, Yasmina Iro knows a thing or two about putting on the mileage. They can often be found exploring the world, traveling to learn about new cultures and experience our beautiful planet. From their home base in the United States, they enjoy creating new worlds and cultures for their readers to explore with them. When not exploring, Yasmina can be found decorating beautiful cakes in their kitchen while caring for their blooming family or sneaking some work on their webcomics. There's always something new going on with them and that's the way they like it. You can connect with Yasmina on their website: www.yasminairo.com